Tackle Without a Team

Books by Matt Christopher

Sports Stories
The Lucky Baseball Bat
Baseball Pals
Basketball Sparkplug
Little Lefty
Touchdown for Tommy
Break for the Basket
Baseball Flyhawk
Catcher with a Glass Arm
The Counterfeit Tackle
Miracle at the Plate
The Year Mom Won the
   Pennant
The Basket Counts
Catch That Pass!
Shortstop from Tokyo
Jackrabbit Goalie
The Fox Steals Home
Johnny Long Legs
Look Who's Playing First Base
Tough to Tackle
The Kid Who Only Hit Homers
Face-Off
Mystery Coach
Ice Magic
No Arm in Left Field
Jinx Glove
Front Court Hex
The Team That Stopped Moving
Glue Fingers

The Pigeon with the Tennis
   Elbow
The Submarine Pitch
Power Play
Football Fugitive
Johnny No Hit
Soccer Halfback
Diamond Champs
Dirt Bike Racer
The Dog That Called the
   Signals
The Dog That Stole Football
   Plays
Drag-Strip Racer
Run, Billy, Run
Tight End
The Twenty-One-Mile Swim
Wild Pitch
Dirt Bike Runaway
The Great Quarterback
   Switch
Supercharged Infield
The Hockey Machine
Red-Hot Hightops
Tackle Without a Team
Animal Stories
Desperate Search
Stranded
Earthquake
Devil Pony

TACKLE WITHOUT A TEAM

MATT CHRISTOPHER

Illustrated by
Margaret Sanfilippo

LITTLE, BROWN AND COMPANY
Boston   Toronto   London

First edition

The characters and events portrayed in this book are ficti-
tious. Any similarities to real persons, living or dead, are co-
incidental and not intended by the author.

Library of Congress Cataloging-in-Publication Data
Christopher, Matt.
    Tackle without a team / Matt Christopher; illustrated by
Margaret Sanfilippo.
        p.   cm.
    Summary: Unjustly dismissed from the football team for drug
possession, Scott learns that only by finding out who planted
the marijuana in his duffel bag can he clear himself with his
parents.
    ISBN 0-316-14067-8
    [1. Football — Fiction.   2. Drugs — Fiction.   3. Mystery and
detective stories.]   I. Sanfilippo, Margaret, ill.   II. Title.
PZ7.C458Tac   1989
[Fic] — dc19
                                                            88-22644
                                                            CIP
                                                            AC

10   9   8   7   6   5   4   3

VB

Published simultaneously in Canada
by Little, Brown & Company (Canada) Limited
Printed in the United States of America

to Joe and Kathy

TACKLE WITHOUT A TEAM

ONE

"Seventeen Fly," Rick Seaver said.

He clapped his hands once. The huddle broke, and all eleven football players scampered to their positions on the dry, sunbaked field.

"Down! Set!"

Red and gray uniforms, most of them still clean and unsmudged, and matching helmets flashed before Scott Kramer's eyes as he crouched down, dug his toes into the turf in his right tackle spot, and faced the tackle in front of him. Left tackle Joe Salerno's eyes, peering through his metal face mask, were like two dark, white-rimmed holes.

The Royals were leading by a narrow margin, 14–13. It was the middle of the second quarter, the ball was the Greyhawks' on their own nine yard line, and it was first down. Unless Rick could pull off the 17 Fly play, or any play he might think of in the next three downs, the Royals had a good chance of pushing that score up by another six or seven points.

"Brace up, Kramer." Joe's low-pitched remark sounded like a snarl. "I'm going to throw you for a loss."

Scott smiled. Ever since the game had started, the broad-shouldered left tackle had tried to intimidate him with sarcastic remarks but never managed to do what he said he'd do.

"You talk too much, Joe," Scott said.

"Hep! Hep! Hep!" Rick barked.

The ball was snapped. Both teams rushed toward each other across the scrimmage line. Helmets and shoulder pads clashed, breaths heaved. Scott could hear his own and Joe Salerno's as he ducked low and to the side in an effort to stop Joe from getting through to Rick. Only once had Joe been able to do so, and that

4

was because Scott had slipped on the grass and lost control of the defensive tackle.

The 17 Fly was a pass play. It required Rick, the quarterback, to turn halfway around with the ball, fake a handoff to a running back behind him — which, in this case, was Monk Robertson — then fade back and heave a pass to the right end, Squint Oliver, who would be crisscrossing down the field to the far left.

Protecting Squint from the Royals' backfield defense would be Karl Draper and Kear Nguyen, left tight end and running back respectively. The play had worked early in the first quarter, putting the Greyhawks in a position to score their first touchdown. This was only the second time that Rick had called for it. Coach Tom Dresso had advised him not to call it too often. "No sense in letting the opposition catch on to your plays," he'd said.

Scott managed to hold off Joe long enough for the play to be executed, and the roar from the crowd told him it had worked. But not for a touchdown. Squint had caught Rick's pass on their twenty-eight yard line and managed to run to the forty-one before the Royals' safety man tackled him.

First down and ten.

Scott met Kear coming toward him, and they exchanged high fives.

"What're you doing after the game?" Kear asked, his eyes smiling through his face mask. He was fourteen, an inch taller than Scott, and thinner.

"Nothing special," Scott answered. "Got something in mind?"

"Yeah. A hot fudge sundae!" Kear laughed.

"Good idea," Scott said, smacking his lips. "You treating?"

"Me? On my stinky income?" Kear laughed again. "I'll settle for a plain chocolate ice cream cone."

Scott grinned. "Me, too."

"Huddle!" Rick's voice cut into their idle chatter.

The two friends turned and headed toward the quarterback, who stood, legs straddled, behind the line of scrimmage.

"Okay, guys," Rick said as the team huddled. "Powerhouse Left."

"About time," Monk grunted.

Rick grinned at the running back who doubled as linebacker on defense. "Put us across the border, Monk," he said, then clapped his hands. "Let's go!"

The team broke from the huddle, scrambled to the line of scrimmage, and once again Scott found himself face-to-face with the Royals' defensive tackle, Joe Salerno.

"Coming this way, right?" Joe said, trying to guess the upcoming play.

Scott's expression didn't change. "Keep guessing, Joe," he said.

Rick's voice boomed through the silence. "Hep! Hep! Hep!"

Lenny Baccus centered the ball. Rick grabbed it, turned, and handed it off to Monk. The burly fullback headed for a hole that was barely wide enough for a sheet of paper to pass through. A pair of hands circled his waist and brought him down for no gain.

"Come on, Bill!" Monk barked at the big right guard as he scrambled to his feet. "You watching this game or playing it?"

Bill Lowry, his eyes like lead balls, looked at

him but said nothing. He seldom did. Sometimes Scott almost felt sorry for him. Bill took
a lot of gaff.

Second and still ten.

"How about Powerhouse Right?" Scott suggested in the huddle as he looked at Rick. "I
think I can handle Salerno."

"I got a better idea," Monk cut in. "Powerhouse Left Option."

Rick's gaze shot to him and back to Scott.
"You guys forget? I'm calling the shots. Okay?"

"Sorry," Scott said.

Monk said nothing.

"Twenty-seven Zero," Rick said.

"All *right!*" Kear exclaimed, grinning.

Standing beside Scott, he slapped Scott on
the rump as the team broke out of the huddle.

"Watch me. This is my play — maybe," he
said, his teeth white and shiny, as he displayed
his familiar grin.

Scott laughed. "Maybe" meant that Kear might
not even get to carry the ball. It depended on
what Rick's chances were of carrying it through
the liz (left) side of the line himself.

Rick barked signals. The ball was snapped.

8

As the option play began to take form, Scott lunged at Joe Salerno for a shoulder block. But this time Joe faked Scott out, diving low under his right arm, scrambling on his knees for a yard or so, then getting to his feet and bolting after Rick. Rick, pulling the ball under his right arm, started to sprint around left end.

Scott turned in time to see Joe reach for him, grab Rick's right leg, and stop him on the spot for a two-yard loss.

A roar burst from the Royals' fans as the referee took the ball from Rick and spotted it on the Greyhawks' thirty-nine yard line.

"Where were you on *that* play, Kramer?" Monk snarled. "He went through you like water through a sieve."

Scott fumed but said nothing. What was there to say? He knew he had goofed. He had under-estimated the Royals' tackle. But what really got under his skin was Monk's sarcasm. The guy seemed to thrive on insults. And anybody was his target.

"He should've passed it off to me," Kear said quietly to Scott. "I went right by him, expecting he would. But he didn't."

9

Scott nodded. "The way the play went, I wish he had, too," he agreed.

They joined the other team members in the huddle.

"Sorry, Rick," Scott said to the quarterback. "My fault."

Rick offered no comment. He called for a pass play — a throw that crisscrossed the field from left to right, almost the exact opposite of the 17 Fly.

The teams got to the line of scrimmage. Signals were called. The ball was snapped.

Rick feinted a pass toward the left side of the field, then heaved a spiraling pass to the tight end, Squint Oliver. Daren Gibson, playing safety for the Royals, leaped, grabbed the ball out of Squint's hands, and headed toward the open field. Scott saw the play after he shoulder-blocked Salerno, then bounced his right shoulder off a linebacker who, off balance, dropped to the ground.

"Oh, no!" Scott murmured as he saw Daren racing toward the sideline, his legs churning like pistons. Without a second thought he started to sprint after the goal-heading runner.

Scott lunged at him on the thirty-six and knocked him out of bounds on the thirty-three, spilling Daren onto the green grass behind the white border line before falling down on it himself.

Daren got up, giving Scott a dirty look, as if Scott had done him an injustice by not letting him continue on for a touchdown. Scott ignored him. He was used to that kind of look. No use letting it get under his skin.

Coach Dresso sent in four new replacements; he had no more. Pete Waner and Moose Gordon replaced Rick and Kear in the backfield. Sid Seaver, Rick's brother, and Ray Hunter replaced Scott and Roy Austin on the line. Scott didn't mind. He was soaked with sweat and bushed. He could use the rest.

The game resumed for two and a half more minutes before a whistle shrilled, ending the first half. The score remained 14–13 in the Royals' favor.

"Well, we're holding them," Kear said, as he and Scott headed off the field together toward the red-brick building that housed the locker rooms.

"So far, anyway," Scott said a little dubiously. A one-point lead could go a long way in this football game. The Royals were tough.

They filed in with the other Greyhawks and Royals players through the narrow pathway between the grandstand and the bleachers to their respective locker rooms.

Scott and Kear removed their helmets and shoes and rested in a corner of the locker room. Sitting on the bare floor may not have been as comfortable as sitting on a bench, but it felt cooler.

"Bill, a little more aggressiveness out of you, okay?" Coach Dresso said to the chunky guard as he launched into his intermission speech to the team. "Sometimes I wonder if you've got steel nuggets for toes."

The guys laughed. Bill Lowry smiled slightly. It was hard for Scott to tell how seriously Bill took criticism.

"Scott, nice tackling. Keep up the good work."

"Yay, Scott," Monk Robertson sneered, just loud enough for Scott to hear.

"Yeah," Roy Austin chipped in.

Scott fumed a little as he pretended he didn't hear them.

"Chuck, you're holding your head too high," the coach went on. "Keep it down."

He said something else to the husky left guard, but Scott wasn't listening anymore. His attention was on the looks and remarks coming from some of the players.

Boy! Try to put in a one-hundred-and-ten percent effort, and they look at you as if you're a hot dog!

He was glad when the fifteen-minute intermission was up.

Monk kicked off to start the second half. Glenn Patch, one of the Royals running backs, caught the ball on their twenty-nine and galloped like a gazelle to the Greyhawks' thirty-three, where Scott knocked him out of bounds.

The ref spotted the ball, blew his whistle, and the teams took their positions at the line of scrimmage. This time Scott found himself facing a different opponent. Buck Logan was bigger, heavier, and tougher than Salerno. His dark eyes stared intently into Scott's.

Bus Barr, the Royals' quarterback, grunted the signals. The ball was put into play. Scott faked a run to Logan's left side, forcing Logan to head in that direction, then quickly reversed his move and shot toward the hole Logan had opened up for him. Logan tried to dive back, reaching for Scott's left shoulder to stop his forward drive, but Scott was already through and on his way after the quarterback.

Barr had handed the ball off to a running back, Jack Lake, who was just beginning to make a sweeping dash around his right end when Scott dove at him. It was a five-yard loss, putting the Royals back on the Greyhawks' thirty-eight.

"Nice break, Scott," Rick said from the sidelines. He didn't smile as he said it, as if it were routine.

Second down and fifteen.

This time Buck seemed to anticipate Scott's move as the ball was snapped from center. He bolted in front of Scott hardly a fraction of a second later, his elbows leveled out straight,

14

pushing Scott back until he lost his balance and fell.

Just before Scott went down he had a glimpse of the ball sailing over his head against the backdrop of blue, cloud-speckled sky. A moment later, a roar broke from the Royals' fans, and Scott knew that a pass had gone for either a long gain or a touchdown.

When he was back on his feet he discovered, disappointedly, that it *was* a touchdown. Royals 20, Greyhawks 13.

He saw Buck Logan's humiliating smile. "Got you that time, old buddy, didn't I?" he said.

"Yeah," Scott said. "Yeah, you sure did."

Monk headed toward Scott as the teams lined up for the Royals' point-after attempt. He was fuming.

"You looked lousy on that play, Kramer." He spit the words out like pebbles. "Maybe you're tired. Maybe you ought to warm the pines for a while."

TWO

Scott's nerves sizzled as if hit with an electric charge. One guy he wished he knew how to cope with was Monk Robertson.

Jack Lake kicked for the extra point and sent the ball sailing just inside the left goalpost to increase the Royals' lead to 21–13.

Scott watched the numbers change on the electric scoreboard on the north side of the field — the Greyhawks' side — and felt that he was as much responsible for the Royals' lead as any of the backfielders were. Maybe more. If he'd gotten through the line, he would've had an excellent chance of tackling Barr. He was fast. Perhaps the fastest lineman the Greyhawks had. Coach Dresso had even played him in the backfield a couple of times but decided he was more useful on the line. Scott was glad of that. It was fun trying to dodge the opposing player, bust through the line, and bring down the ball-carrier. You didn't always succeed; no one *always* did. But when you did succeed, it made you feel good all over.

Heading back across the field to prepare for the kickoff, Scott removed his helmet and mask and sponged the sweat off his forehead with the sleeve of his jersey. He heard the sound of pounding feet grow louder behind him, and he turned to see Kear returning to the game.

"Coming back in to bring us out of this mess?" Scott said, trying to force a grin.

"Somebody's got to do it," Kear answered. His eyes narrowed. "Hey, I saw Monk giving you some lip. Why don't you talk back to the bigmouth?"

"Why should I?" Scott replied, pulling his helmet and mask back on. "That would just bring me down to his level."

Kear looked at him and nodded. "Yeah, I

guess you're right. Let the bigmouth have his fun. He'll get what's coming to him someday."

Jack Lake kicked off for the Royals. The ball sailed end-over-end across the fifty yard line to the corner slot, where Elmo George caught it against his chest and bolted up the field to the Greyhawks' thirty-nine yard line.

Rick called for a draw play, which went for a four-yard gain. A play through left tackle, where Roy Austin had replaced Sid Seaver, resulted in one more.

Third and five. The ball was on the Greyhawks' forty-four yard line.

"Twenty-seven Op Fly," Rick ordered in the huddle.

The play required Rick to take the centered ball and hand it off to Monk, who would fake a run toward the left side of the line, then heave a pass to Kear, who would be racing behind the line of scrimmage to the right side and down into Royals territory.

Again Scott found himself looking into Joe Salerno's strong, grim face and penny-sized eyes. He listened to Rick call the signals. On the third

"Hep!" he ducked quickly and bolted forward, hitting Joe with his right shoulder and sending the Royals' tackle skidding backward on his rump.

Scott sprinted past the encumbered player, briefly catching a glimpse of Joe's surprised, angry face, and headed toward the flanker, whose darting glances at the Greyhawks' backfield seemed confused. He didn't see Scott until almost the last second. By then Scott was on him with a block that put him out of commission long enough for Kear to be in the clear for Monk's pass.

It worked for a sixteen-yard gain. Only the Royals' safety was between Kear and the goal line, and he managed to tackle Kear on their forty.

"Nice play, you guys!" Rick exclaimed happily, as the team huddled. "Let's try it again — only this time we'll go the rip side."

Scott noted that nothing was said about his block. But, he guessed "Nice play, you guys!" included him. Anyway, he tried to forget it as he hustled to his right tackle position.

This time Monk was to run to the right, pass off to Elmo, and Elmo was to heave the bomb to the left tight end, Karl Draper.

It didn't work. Elmo's pass was short and almost caught by a defensive back.

It took the next three downs for the Greyhawks to make a move, and they did it on a through-tackle play on Scott's side of the line. Kear took the ball for a gain that put them within six yards of the goal line.

First and goal. Monk bucked the line for two yards, then bucked it again for another two. Kear tried to put the ball across on the third down but was smothered when he got within a yard.

"Let me take it," Monk said, his breath heaving as he fastened his eyes on Rick. "I'll put it across. I know I will."

Rick was hesitant. "Their line is strong," he said. "It's like a brick wall."

"Let him carry it," Scott cut in. "Behind me. I'll open up a hole for him."

Monk met Scott's eyes briefly. Then, as if he hadn't heard him, Monk said to Rick, "I'm thinking about jumping over center."

"You sure you can do it?" Rick said, eyeing Monk sharply.

"Would I say I would if I couldn't?" Monk retorted.

Rick grinned. "Okay. Let's go."

The team hustled to the scrimmage line. Rick barked signals, got the centered ball, turned and handed it off to Monk.

A thunderous sound exploded from the Royals' line as it broke forward to stop the on-rushing, leaping backfield man. Monk was up in the air for a moment — hovering like a big, wounded bird — and didn't gain an inch. The ball went to the Royals on the one yard line.

"He should've done what you said," Kear muttered disgustedly to Scott as they rose up slowly from the turf and waited for the ref to spot the ball. "He would've made it."

"For some stupid reason that guy doesn't like me," Scott said, clamping his jaws together.

"Stupid is right," Kear agreed. "Anybody who doesn't like you must be stupid."

Scott grinned. "Thanks, ol' pal."

The whistle shrieked, and the teams lined up at the one yard line.

21

The signals were called, the ball was snapped. Bus took it and faded back. Scott, tearing through the narrow hole between Joe and the left guard, Willie Montgomery, pounced on the unaware quarterback and brought him down in the end zone for a safety! Two points!

Royals 21, Greyhawks 15.

"Hey, nice play!" said Kear.

Scott smiled. "Oh, you noticed," he said, brushing off his smudged sleeves.

"I noticed, too," Rick said, coming up beside him. "Good play."

"Good play?" Kear echoed. "Is that all you can say? It was a *fantastical* good play! Give the guy credit, Rick!"

Rick glared at him. "I *am* giving him credit. What do you want me to do — cartwheels?" He socked Kear lightly on the shoulder. "Let's go. We're still trailing by six points."

It was obvious to Scott that Rick wasn't as impressed by his tackle as Kear was. But then, Kear was a good friend. He would naturally feel more impressed.

The ball was spotted on the Royals' forty yard line and Daren Gibson kicked off. Moose

Gordon, taking Monk's place in the backfield, caught the end-over-end boot on the Greyhawks' thirty-two and made a wide sweep to the forty-three before he was brought down.

The Greyhawks had time for two more plays — advancing the ball into Royals' territory to their forty-nine — when the quarter ended.

Third and two.

Moose bucked the line for a yard gain. Fourth and one.

"What now, chief?" Moose said in the huddle, his face shining with sweat behind his face mask. "Shall I buck it again?"

"Kick it," said Lenny.

"Yeah, kick it," agreed Bill Lowry.

"Why not try something they won't expect?" Scott cut in. "Like a pass."

Rick looked at him. He said nothing for a moment, then nodded. "Good idea. You ends," he said, addressing Karl Draper and Squint Oliver, "flare out and watch for a bomb. On two. Let's go!"

He clapped his hands once, and the huddle

broke. The players formed at the line of scrimmage, and on the second "Hep!" Lenny Baccus centered the ball to Rick. Rick faded back as the linemen plunged forward. Scott made sure he was performing his job again: keeping tackle Joe Salerno busy until Rick could get his pass off. But, unless left tackle Roy Austin and the guards did their jobs, too, Rick would be pulled down, and the ball would go to the Royals.

The play worked. Rick delivered a pass to Squint down the right side of the field, and Squint galloped for twenty-two yards for a touchdown. Moose kicked the extra point, and the Greyhawks went into the lead, 22–21.

"Hey, guess you called that play right," Kear said to Scott, as the teams headed to their respective positions on the field. "Maybe you ought to sub as quarterback."

"With my weak arm?" Scott laughed. "No way!"

His arm wasn't all that weak, but he'd had his chance in the backfield and liked the line better. He enjoyed blocking the opposing tackle and breaking through to pull down the quarterback. And someone had to do it.

The ball changed possession several times during the remainder of the quarter, but at no time were the Royals a real threat again. The game ended with the Greyhawks winning, 22–21.

The teams, both tired and sweat-drenched, trudged to their respective locker rooms. Scott fell to the floor in front of his locker to rest before he took a shower.

"Pooped out, ol' boy?" said Kear, his sweat-drenched hair hanging over his forehead and ears.

Scott's chest rose and fell as he heaved a sigh of relief. "No. Dead," he said.

He closed his eyes and relaxed, feeling a tingle in his muscles and joints. He got a kick out of the action on the field, but he was always glad when the game was over. Football was one sport that left you drained and achy.

"Oo, lookee here!" Elmo's voice cut in. "The great tackle, Scott Kramer, is all fagged out and is going to take a little bitty nap before he goes home. Tsk! Tsk!"

That did it.

"Jeez!" Scott cried, jerking to his elbows and

25

glaring at the halfback as he headed to his locker. "A guy can't shut his eyes two seconds without some wise guy getting on his case."

Elmo laughed.

So did Kear. "Might as well shower," he said. "Nobody's going to let you rest."

"Right."

Scott got to his feet — slowly — opened his locker and lifted out his wrinkled black duffel bag. Unzipping it, he saw something that made his eyes pop and brought goosebumps to his skin. . . .

Lying on top of a towel were two hand-rolled cigarettes. *Marijuana.* He'd seen it before.

But they weren't his. He didn't smoke. Not grass, not anything. And any team member caught possessing cigarettes — of *any* kind — was *kicked off immediately*.

Whose were they, and why were they in his duffel bag?

As if his hands had suddenly taken over his senses, Scott picked up the joints, still staring at them as if hypnotized.

"Put 'em back, idiot!" a voice whispered

sharply. "You want to get caught with those? They're dynamite, man!"

The voice was Kear Nguyen's.

Quickly, Scott stuck them underneath the towel, his hand still shaking uncontrollably.

"What was that?" another voice cut in from behind him.

Scott glanced over his shoulder and saw Coach Dresso. He had just come around the row of lockers and was looking down at the duffel bag.

"N-nothing," Scott breathed, as his stomach flip-flopped.

THREE

"Nothing? Then why are your hands shaking?" the coach asked.

He stepped up beside Scott, towering above him like the Jolly Green Giant.

Scott didn't move. Didn't speak. He was frozen.

"Mind letting me see what you're hiding in there?" the coach asked quietly.

Scott hesitated. Then, reluctantly, he unzipped the bag again and took out the towel, revealing the two marijuana cigarettes underneath.

"They're — they're not mine," he stammered, nervous and worried.

The coach stared at him. "You mean to tell me somebody *else* put those in there?"

Sweating profusely, Scott nodded.

Coach Dresso cleared his throat. "I wish I could believe you, Scott," he said. "But if that was true, then why did you try to hide them again? Why didn't you bring them to me right away?"

"I guess I wasn't thinking straight. I was surprised. But I swear, I don't smoke the stuff," Scott insisted.

"Let me have them," the coach said, extending his hand.

Scott handed the marijuana to him, praying that the coach believed him.

"After you shower and get into your civvies, I want to talk with you," the coach said and moved on.

Scott stared after him, his heart still beating like crazy. He felt eyes on him now and glanced quickly around to see every pair in the room staring at him. I know what they're thinking, he thought. My brother, Eddie, had smoked dope. He'd even gotten caught with it in his car and arrested. They probably think I'm just like him. But I could never let that happen to me!

Kear looked at him, stunned. "You smoke grass?"

"No! You *know* I don't!" Scott exclaimed, his voice low but strained. "Somebody else put those joints in there!"

"Who?"

"How the heck would I know?"

Choking back tears, he zipped up the duffel bag, got up, and started to head toward the coach's office.

"Scott." Kear grabbed his arm. "I believe you."

Scott's mouth tightened. Then he said, "Thanks," and kept walking, feeling as though he were going to his execution.

"Aren't you going to shower?" Coach Dresso asked when Scott walked in.

"No. I'll wait until I get home," Scott replied. "You wanted to tell me something?"

The coach nodded. "Yes, as much as I hate to." He sighed deeply. "I don't know what else to do but tell it to you straight, Scott. You know the rules. I don't condone ordinary cigarette smoking for any athlete, and certainly not for

31

kids your age. And marijuana" — the coach's tone grew sharper — "that's an illegal substance, in case you'd forgotten."

"I told you, I don't smoke, Coach," Scott said stiffly. "Not even regular cigarettes."

"But I have evidence to the contrary, Scott."

"I know. But you've got to believe me, Coach," Scott insisted. "I didn't put those joints in there. Somebody else did."

"All right. Who? Only somebody who doesn't like you. And there isn't a guy on the team who fits that description."

Monk Robertson does, Scott wanted to say. But he didn't have any proof to back up his feeling.

"No," the coach continued. "I can't think of a single person on the team who would be nasty enough to plant them in your duffel. As far as I know right now, those joints are yours. You probably purchased them sometime between now and the last time you showered, stuck them into your duffel bag, and forgot all about it."

Scott's eyes ached as he stared at the coach. "I didn't —" he started to say.

"And you've got to pay the penalty," the coach

went on, ignoring Scott's interruption. "I'd really like to believe you, Scott, but if I just let you off the hook like that, it wouldn't be a very good example to the other players, would it?"

Scott didn't answer.

"Anyway, as of now, you're off the team. Sorry, Scott, but that's the rule. Given the seriousness of this incident, I should also inform the principal and your parents, but since —"

Scott whirled around and ran out the door, as the remainder of the coach's words faded into silence behind him.

The principal! And his parents . . . Eddie's arrest had shamed them no end. He couldn't let them go through that misery again!

"All because someone stashed their pot in my bag!" he whispered, hurt and angry. "Why did they pick on me?"

He stormed out of the locker room to the wide, bush-lined walkway where more than a dozen kids were waiting for their friends to emerge. They all stared at him, puzzled.

"Why didn't you take a shower?" several of them asked almost in unison.

He didn't answer but continued on toward

the parking lot where his parents and sisters — Anna Mae, eleven, and Carolyn, nine — were waiting for him. Only Eddie wasn't there. He was attending his first year of college. I wonder what he'd think, or say, if he were here now, Scott thought. He'd been through it. But with him it was real. He *had* smoked marijuana. He *knew* what it was like to get caught and be guilty.

Suddenly, two girls broke away from the group and rushed toward him, stopping in front of him so that he couldn't take another step.

"Scott!" murmured Jerilea Townsend, a brown-eyed brunette he'd come to like since the eighth grade. "You look as if you lost the game, not won it! What happened?"

"I've just been fired," Scott said solemnly and pushed on between them.

"Fired?" Fran Whitaker echoed, her eyes flashing wide. "What do you mean . . . *fired*?" Fran was a friend of Kear's.

"Just what I said," Scott answered, trying not to sound belligerent but not really caring whether he did or not. Uppermost in his mind was the thought that the coach was wrong in kicking him off the team. Just because those cigarettes were in his duffel bag didn't prove a thing. *Anybody* could have put them in there. The locker door hadn't been locked, nor had his duffel bag.

He heard the clatter of the girls' shoes as they ran to keep up with him. "Scott! Aren't you going to tell us what happened? Why were you fired?" Jerilea asked, her voice shrill.

"The coach saw a couple of cigarettes in my duffel bag." Scott chose not to mention what *kind* of cigarettes. He didn't want word to get around that he had been caught with drugs. "I don't smoke, and I told him so. I told him somebody must have stuck 'em in there, but he wouldn't believe me."

"That's not *fair*!" Jerilea cried.

Tell me about it, Scott thought to himself as he kept on walking. The girls didn't follow him this time.

He was relieved. He was embarrassed enough without having them around to see him wallow in his frustration.

He reached the tan, four-door car where his

parents and the girls were waiting, tossed the bag onto the floor in back, and plunked himself down next to Anna Mae.

"Okay! Let's go!" he said, forcing a grin and pretending nothing was bothering him. He had decided to keep mum. He knew the effect it would have on them if they knew what had happened. They'd be crushed.

Carolyn stared at him. "You didn't shower," she observed, wrinkling her nose.

She *would* have to notice that, he thought. "I didn't want to keep all of you waiting," he explained.

His father started up the car.

"Something wrong?" his mother asked, looking back at him. "I don't remember your not taking a shower right after a game before."

His fists tightened. "Oh, Ma. Nothing's wrong. Can't I skip a shower just once without everybody giving me the third degree?"

He glanced at the rearview mirror and saw his father looking at him, too. If anybody could tell when something was troubling him, it was his father.

But all Mr. Kramer said was, "Okay, okay.

Let's leave the boy alone. He played a good game and must be tired."

Scott breathed a sigh of relief.

But, as they headed out of the parking lot, the hurt feeling came back stronger than ever. They'd find out the truth sooner or later, he thought. They had to — the next time the Greyhawks played, and he didn't suit up.

He couldn't remember being in a worse mess in his life.

FOUR

It was shortly after four o'clock when Scott got a phone call from Kear.

"What're you up to?" Kear asked.

"Watching some dumb movie," Scott answered, staring at the TV screen that was in front of him and Anna Mae. He hadn't been able to concentrate on the story, anyway. The earlier events of the day still plagued him. And being around his sisters and parents made him uneasy. He was afraid that at any moment one of them would start asking him questions again. *Out with it, Scott. What happened back there in the locker room?* He couldn't quite face that yet.

"Scott?"

38

"Yeah?"

"If you want me to, I'll quit the team," Kear said.

"What? No way! Are you crazy?"

"I'm your friend," Kear said softly. "And I think it's rotten what the coach did to you."

"You're not going to quit —" Scott blurted, before he remembered his sister was within earshot, and took the phone to another room. "You're not quitting the team," he continued, a little more softly. "I know how much you love to play football."

He couldn't believe it. Kear was really a close friend, to be willing to quit football for him.

"I don't love it any more than you do," Kear said. "What are you going to do?"

"I don't know," Scott said, shrugging his shoulders. "Maybe I can find some other team to play on. But if the word gets around about me, I'm dead. I'm like the guy in that book, *The Man Without a Country*. Only I'm the kid without a football team."

Kear laughed. Scott laughed, too. But only for a moment. Being without a football team was not very funny.

"Hey," Kear went on, his mood changed for the better, "want to see a *real* movie?"

"Sure," said Scott. "No matter what it is, it's got to be better than this mushy stuff."

Kear chuckled. "It's about ghosts, so it *must* be better."

Scott grinned. "Right. What time do you want to go?"

"The movie starts at six," Kear said. "A quarter of six okay?"

"Wait a sec," Scott said. He clamped a hand over the mouthpiece of the telephone and yelled, "Ma! Okay if I go to a movie with Kear?"

"When? And what's the movie?" his mother's high-pitched voice came from the kitchen.

"It's about a ghost! And it starts at six!"

"Ghost? No way! You have enough nightmares already without going to a horror movie! Tell Kear —"

"Oh, Ma!" Scott interrupted, disappointed. "What's one more nightmare? I live through them all right, don't I?"

There was a pause. The next minute he heard a tapping on wood. He turned and saw her standing on the wide threshold separating the dining and living rooms, tapping the handle part of a knife against the casing. Her blue-eyed gaze was fastened on him.

"*You* live through them," she said. "But maybe the next time *I* won't. You frighten me half to death with your jumping up in bed and gasping for air. And you want to see a horror movie?"

He nodded, smiling. "Yeah."

She shook her blonde head, gave the casing a sharp tap with the knife handle, and headed back to the kitchen. "Okay. Go ahead," she said. "I guess I can live through another nightmare, too."

Scott laughed. "Thanks, Ma!" He took his hand off the mouthpiece of the telephone and said into it, "See you at a quarter of six, Kear."

Scott plunked back down on the easy chair he'd been sitting on and continued to watch the movie. It got more boring by the minute; it seemed that all the main actor and actress did was talk and kiss. Finally, he couldn't stand it any longer and went to his room to read.

Kear arrived a few minutes early, but Scott was ready. His mother suggested that he take his red jacket along because, by the time the movie let out, the temperature might drop a few degrees.

They started to walk the five blocks to Cinema 4, where the movie was playing. As they were about to cross to the second block, Scott saw two girls on the next corner, waiting for a bus. Even from where he stood he could see that they were smoking.

He grabbed Kear's hand. "Hold it a second," he said.

They paused on the curb.

"Isn't that Peg Moore and Flossie the Glossie?" Kear said, staring up the street at the girls.

"Yeah."

"Isn't Peg the one you once had a crush on?" Kear went on.

"Don't remind me," Scott said. Just the same, his mind reverted back to the not-too-distant past when he and Peg Moore had been a couple. It didn't last long, because he'd found out she smoked — sometimes even marijuana. And she'd only been twelve then, a couple of months younger than he.

He didn't think that anyone should smoke. Especially not pot. Maybe it was because of his parents' strict rule or Eddie's experience that he felt this way, but when he'd found out Peg smoked, he hardly ever saw or spoke to her again.

The girl with her, Florence Menkin — who most of the kids called Flossie the Glossie, because she wore so much makeup — smoked, too.

"Oh, no. They spotted us," Scott groaned.

Flossie the Glossie was waving to them. "Scott! Kear! Come here!" she called.

"We don't *have* to go, do we?" said Scott, afraid of what to expect from them. Peg, especially.

"Well, we have to go that way to get to the theater," Kear said.

Reluctantly, Scott followed Kear to the corner where the girls were standing. He didn't have to get too close to recognize the odor of marijuana.

"Hi, guys," Florence said. "Where're you headed?"

"The movies," Kear answered. Scott frowned at him. What was he going to do next, invite them along? he thought.

But Peg hardly seemed to notice Kear. She

was smiling and peering at Scott with her bloodshot eyes. Slowly she lifted her arm and held the joint out to him.

"Want a puff?" she drawled.

Scott blushed. "No, thanks."

"Why not? I thought you'd finally come to your senses and turned on to it."

It dawned on Scott that, despite his efforts to keep it quiet, Peg must have heard about his being kicked off the team because of marijuana. Now she was rubbing it in.

Kear must have come to the same conclusion. "Who told you that?" he demanded.

"Come on, Kear, let's go," Scott said, pulling his friend's arm. He wanted to say, *She's not worth the trouble. She's not kidding anyone but herself.*

He was glad to hear the sound of the bus as it came around the corner and pulled up to the curb. The girls took one last drag — as if their lives depended on it — and then dropped the cigarettes to the ground before climbing onto the bus.

"See you!" Florence said.

Peg just smiled and waved, like a movie star-let in one of those magazine ads.

The bus roared off.

"I wonder . . ." Scott whispered tensely. "She smokes dope, and she seemed to know about what happened . . ." He faltered. No, he thought. She couldn't be the one.

He felt Kear looking intently at him.

"I can't believe she'd pull a dirty trick on me just to get even," he said, his voice thin. "Could you, Kear?"

Kear stared at him. "Even for what?"

"For breaking off — you know — our friend-ship."

Kear shrugged. "Who knows? She's a tough cookie. Maybe she would, maybe she wouldn't. Some girls would do *anything* to get even with a guy."

Scott grinned. "You sound as if you know a lot about girls."

Kear shrugged again. "I'm an expert. I've got one sister and a girlfriend. Well, I figure she's a girlfriend."

"One sister and Fran Whitaker?" Scott

laughed. "I've got *two* sisters and a girlfriend. Guess I'm one-girl more expert than you are. Let's go, before the movie starts."

They headed up the street, walking a little faster now.

"It sure is a coincidence, though," Scott said, before they had gone a full block. "Don't you think?"

"That it's a coincidence? Sure. Like the cops say on TV: It's a real *strong* coincidence!"

They arrived at the theater early, bought a bag of buttered popcorn each, and ate it while they waited for the movie to start.

Scott couldn't get Peg out of his thoughts. If anybody had the motive — and the guts — to stick a couple of joints in his duffel bag, it was she. But how could he prove it? She wouldn't confess to it, and buddy-buddy Florence sure wouldn't snitch on her, if she even knew about it.

The movie started, but Scott might as well have stayed home. He couldn't concentrate on this movie, either. He just kept thinking about Peg, about Coach Dresso catching him with the marijuana, and about his not telling his family.

He felt lousy, angry, and guilty. He wished he could find a hole to crawl into. He'd stay there forever.

He hardly said a word on the way home after the movie. Kear did all the talking. And, from his reaction, the movie must have been exciting. *Too bad I had other things on my mind*, Scott thought.

The minute he stepped into the house, he knew something had happened while he was gone. The expression on his mother's face was like writing on the wall.

"No sense trying to hide that secret from us anymore, Scott," she said firmly. "Your father and I know."

He stared at her, then tromped into the living room and sat down before he fainted. His head suddenly felt light.

"Coach Dresso called," his mother's voice rang like a knell in his ears. "He's coming over to pick up your uniform."

Scott tried to swallow the ache in his throat and asked, "He — he told you what happened?"

"Yes."

His father came into the room. He looked mad enough to smack Scott. But he never had and never would. At least Scott hadn't thought so — before now. "I couldn't believe it, Scott," Mr. Kramer said in a low tone. "Not after what happened to Eddie."

"I didn't put those joints in there, Dad," Scott insisted. "Somebody else did."

"Don't lie to me!" Mr. Kramer suddenly snapped. "You know what I think of lying!"

"I'm not lying, Dad," Scott said evenly, the ache back in his throat again. "It's the truth."

His mother came up beside his father, her hands clasped in front of her. "If you didn't do it, who did? Who would?"

"I — I don't know," he said.

He couldn't tell them he thought that Peg Moore might have done it. He could get in trouble accusing somebody he really wasn't sure about.

"If it wasn't you, why didn't you tell us about the whole thing in the first place?" his father said, his voice still angry.

"I — I don't know," Scott answered. "I guess I didn't want you to . . . to get hurt again."

"Hurt?" his father echoed. "Well, hiding the truth from us certainly didn't help. Because you didn't come to us right away, I don't know whether to believe you. In any case, I think some kind of punishment is in order here. Maybe we should ground you for a couple of weeks."

"I think that being kicked off the team is punishment enough, Ed," Mrs. Kramer said softly.

Scott looked at her gratefully. His father might not believe him, but at least his mother seemed to.

"I don't know," Mr. Kramer said again. "I just hope he's not following in his brother's footsteps."

"Oh, Ed," Mrs. Kramer exclaimed, looking at him. "I'm sure he isn't."

Scott's heart pounded. He felt certain now that no matter what he said, his father wouldn't believe him. Somehow he had to find the person who had put those cigarettes in his duffel

bag. It was the only way he could redeem himself.

It was shortly after supper when Coach Tom
Dresso stopped at the house to pick up Scott's
uniform. Scott answered the door.

"Just a minute," Mrs. Kramer said as Scott
started to head to his room to get it. "I'd like
to talk to Mr. Dresso first."

"Oh, Ma," Scott said.

"Never mind oh Ma-ing me," his mother said
as she rose from the sofa. "I just want to get a
few things straight, that's all."

Sure, Scott thought. And give him a piece of
your mind.

"Shall I get the uniform?" he asked.

"No. Wait. Maybe I can change his mind."

"I doubt it, Ma," he said, trying to be calm —
and keep her calm at the same time.

"I can try," she told him, and headed toward
the door in the foyer. He waited, feeling his
heart thumping against his rib cage again. *Please,
Ma, don't get into an argument with him*, he pleaded
silently.

From where he stood he could see Coach Dresso take off his familiar baseball cap and smile at his mother. The coach said something that Scott couldn't hear.

"Please come inside a minute, will you, Mr. Dresso?" she invited, stepping back so he could enter. She closed the door softly behind him.

"Mr. Dresso," she began, craning her neck up at him — he was about a foot taller than she — "Scott didn't put those marijuana cigarettes in his duffel bag. He doesn't even smoke ordinary cigarettes, let alone that filthy stuff. You can't really think . . ."

"I'm sorry, Mrs. Kramer," the coach interrupted courteously. "But the cigarettes *were* in his bag, and we have a very strict rule —"

"I understand the rule, Mr. Dresso," Mrs. Kramer cut in, keeping her voice soft and her temper under control. "But those cigarettes were put there by somebody else who wanted to incriminate my son. Whether it was another boy on your team or somebody who doesn't even play football, I don't know. But I *know* it wasn't Scott who put them in there."

"Again, Mrs. Kramer, I must say I'm sorry," Coach Dresso said evenly. "Until I can get real proof that Scott didn't put them in there, I must stick to the rules. I saw them in Scott's bag myself. I already told him that I can't give him special treatment." He paused. "One other thing."

She stared at him. "You're not going to remind me about Eddie, are you? That was a long time ago, and he paid for it. Over and over again . . ."

"No, I wasn't going to mention Eddie," the coach said, his glance shifting to Scott. "I was just going to say that at least four of the boys told me that Scott smoked cigarettes at one time. Plain cigarettes. If that's true, he might have been tempted —"

Her eyes flared. "That's ridiculous!"

"Why don't you ask him?" the coach said.

She turned to Scott, her forehead creasing as she fastened her gaze on her son.

"Is that true, Scott? Did you ever smoke cigarettes?"

His heart sank. It *was* true. He could remember the moment clearly, even though it was years ago, when he was nine. It was at night, on Monk Robertson's back porch. Three other kids were with them: Ray Hunter, Jack Whelan, and Bertie McAllister.

"Yes," he admitted, looking straight into her eyes.

Her eyebrows shot up. "Oh, Scott. I thought you said you didn't . . ."

"It was only once! A long time ago. I just took a puff or two," he said in a rush. "That's all. Because I started to cough. I coughed like crazy. And I haven't touched a cigarette since, I swear!"

Mrs. Kramer stared at him a moment longer, her expression indicating that she was still surprised he had taken as much as one puff. She turned back to Coach Dresso.

"Is that what the boys told you?" she asked him.

"Well, I'm afraid not. They said he smoked more than that."

"They lied!" Scott said angrily. "They're a bunch of liars!"

The coach shook his head regretfully. "I really have to go now," he said. "I'm very sorry it turned out like this."

"So am I," Mrs. Kramer said, her voice tinged with bitterness now. "I guess you are definitely off the team, Scott."

Head bowed, Scott trudged up to his room, got his uniform and helmet, and brought them to the coach.

"Sorry about this, Scott," Coach Dresso said sincerely. "But I have no alternative."

"I know," Scott said sadly. He didn't know what else to say.

"Good evening, Mrs. Kramer, Scott," the coach said and left.

Mrs. Kramer closed the door quietly, then walked past Scott without a word and sat down on the sofa.

"I'm sorry, Ma," Scott said, following her into the room. "I'm sorry I never told you."

She took a deep breath and let it out slowly. "I don't expect you to tell me everything. But you've been hiding so much lately, I don't know what to believe anymore."

Even though her voice was gentle, almost resigned, her words stung Scott. Now even his mother doubted him.

Whoever had framed Scott had caused more damage than he or she could ever have imagined.

FIVE

Kear rode his bike over to Scott's house after school the next day. Scott was mowing the lawn, and he shut the motor off as Kear pedaled up the driveway.

"How about going bike riding?" Kear suggested. "That lawn doesn't look like it needs cutting."

Scott paused. No, it doesn't, he thought as he glanced over the large front lawn. But he had to do something to patch things up between him and his father.

"I don't know," he told Kear. He would have liked to go, but then again, he had his father to think about.

"Come on," Kear coaxed. "You can mow that lawn anytime."

Scott thought about that a minute and grinned. "Yeah, I guess you're right," he said. "Be with you in a minute."

He pushed the mower into the garage and took out his bike. Then he and Kear rode out of the driveway and down the street. Scott let Kear take the lead.

They rode in silence. Scott had his eyes on the pavement most of the time, his thoughts on the future football career that had gone up in smoke. There were times he had thought of winning a football scholarship. Maybe those same thoughts were in his father's mind, too. That could explain why he was so angry about what had happened.

Who was the crumb who had put the marijuana into his duffel bag, anyway? And why would he or she do such a lousy thing?

The sound of voices pulled him out of his reverie. He looked up to see that they were riding by the city park, where a bunch of guys were practicing football. Did Kear ride by here on purpose? he asked himself.

"Well, what do you know?" Kear said, stopping at the curb. "A football practice."

Scott pulled up behind him. "I suppose you didn't know about this?"

Kear looked at him and grinned. "Shall we watch them awhile? Maybe we can get a few pointers."

Scott grinned. "Smartmouth," he said.

Kear lifted his bike over the curb, walked it into the park, and stood it up against an oak tree. Scott parked his beside it.

"Who are these guys?" he asked.

"The Cougars," Kear said.

"Cougars? Never heard of them."

"It's a new team — that's why they're not in a league," Kear explained.

Scott looked at him. "How do you know so much about them?"

"A couple of their players live near me," Kear said.

They sat down on a thick root under the comfortable shade of the oak tree and watched the Cougars work out. The players were dressed in worn, smudgy, green uniforms with "Cougars" printed across the front and large num-

bers on the back. A guy about six feet tall, with a crew cut and wearing a gray sweatshirt and pants, was coaching the players.

He was working out with the offense, showing a kid how to take the ball from center, fade back, and heave a pass to a running back. Five players, including a linebacker, formed a defensive line, and five an offensive line, including the center. Another group of players, some twenty feet away, were practicing man-on-man defense.

The scene made Scott nostalgic. He sought out the guards and tackles and saw a big, brawny kid wearing the dirtiest uniform on the field pushing his man back with hardly any resistance. I wonder if he could do that to me, Scott thought. His heart picked up a beat. I would sure love to find out!

He wondered if the team would have a scrimmage; the Greyhawks usually did before they were finished practicing. But the number of players he was watching hardly seemed enough to make up two teams. He counted seventeen members. Twenty-two were needed.

His expectations were fulfilled some ten minutes later when the coach clapped his hands and shouted, "Okay, guys! Scrimmage!" He assigned a bunch of guys to play defense and another group to play offense. In a minute, two lines were formed, each standing facing one another. The defense had nine players, the offense eight.

"Coach! You're short of players — and we're available!"

Kear turned and stared at Scott. His eyes widened. "I don't believe it! *You* said that?"

Scott, his heart pounding, grinned. "Yes," he said. "I said that."

"All ri-i-i-i-ght!" Kear exclaimed.

Scott saw eighteen faces, including the coach's, turn and stare at them.

"You guys play football?" the coach inquired.

"We sure do!" Scott replied, rising to his feet.

He saw no need to explain more at this time. Or anytime. Unless the coach started asking questions.

Kear rose to his feet, too, and stood beside him.

"Okay!" the coach said. "I've got some equipment for you guys in my station wagon. Follow me!"

Scott and Kear followed him to a blue station wagon parked at the curb. The coach opened the back of it, drew out shoulder pads, helmets, and rubber-cleated shoes, and tossed them to Scott and Kear.

"Here. Put them on," he said. "What positions do you kids play?"

"Tackle," Scott said.

"Backfield," Kear said.

"Good." The coach smiled as if he had just discovered a winning combination. "I'll put you on defense," he said to Scott, "and you on offense," to Kear. He offered his hand. "I'm Joe Zacks. Who are you guys?"

The boys told him while they donned their equipment.

"Play on any team?"

"I do. The Greyhawks," Kear answered, casting a side glance at Scott.

"I used to," Scott said. "But now I'm not on any team."

The coach looked at him, then at Kear,

studying their faces. Scott hoped he wouldn't ask many more questions. "Are you sure you know what you're doing? I wouldn't want either of you to risk getting hurt," he said.

"Don't worry about us," Kear said. "We're tough."

"So are the guys out there." The coach pointed at the players watching them from across the field. "Come on. I'll introduce you to my Cougars, and we'll get going."

Scott breathed a sigh of relief as they headed toward the waiting players.

"We're not in a league," Coach Zacks explained. "By the time we formed and got a backer, it was too late to join. But that doesn't mean we're a bunch of hicks. I've got some very good players."

They reached the team members, and Coach Zacks introduced Scott and Kear. By the looks of some of them, Scott didn't doubt what the coach had said. They looked tough. Tougher than nails.

Coach Zacks rattled off the players for the offensive team and then those for the defensive team. He placed Scott at right tackle on the defensive team and Kear at the right halfback position on the offensive team. Grouping up at the scrimmage line, Scott immediately saw that his opponent was Lance Woodlawn, a kid about two inches taller than he. Lance's face was expressionless as he looked at Scott.

On the very first play Lance bolted forward and elbowed Scott in the ribs, knocking Scott flat on his rear.

"That's just a sample, Kramer," he said, smiling as he watched Scott rise slowly to his feet.

Scott gritted his teeth. Okay, pal, he thought. If that's the way you want it, that's the way you'll get it.

SIX

The play was an end-around run that netted the fullback, Barney Stone, seven yards.

Scott prepared himself for Lance's charge on the next play. He couldn't let the taller kid intimidate him, even if this was just a scrimmage and they were on the same team.

"Down! Set! Hut! Hut! Hut!" quarterback Zane Corbett barked.

On the third "Hut!" Lance lunged forward, his elbows stuck out like V-shaped prongs. At the same time, Scott dodged to the side, turning his body to slide through the gap between the opposing tackle and guard.

For the next couple of seconds, Scott avoided being touched, which allowed him to charge ahead and bring down the running back, who had just taken a handoff from Zane. It was a five-yard loss.

"Nice play, Kramer!" Coach Zacks yelled.

Scott resisted the temptation to smile and say thanks. No sense in risking jealousy from team members by being too friendly with the coach, he thought. He was sure he had already spoiled any hopes of being friends with Lance Wood-lawn on that last play.

On the next two plays, Lance was still de-termined to try to block Scott or knock him down. Scott could hear the taller boy's grunting breaths as Lance bore down on him, but Scott always managed to slip away and bolt past him — except once, when the taller boy grabbed his arm and held him.

"That's holding, Lance," Scott said evenly.

"Is it?" Lance snorted and let him go.

They scrimmaged about half an hour longer before Coach Zacks blew his whistle, calling a halt to it.

"You guys did fine," he said to Scott and Kear. "I'd like to have both of you on our team, but I understand that only Scott is available."

He studied the husky, dark-haired boy. "Well, what about it?"

Scott grinned. "Thank you, sir!"

"You must get a physical," Coach Zacks reminded him. "The sooner the better. Then bring a copy of the report to me. The garage that sponsors us will pay for it and also for your insurance, so you won't have to worry about that. Okay. See you tomorrow night — same time, same place."

He started to turn away, then paused and added, "One more thing: take the pads and face mask home with you. I'll have a uniform for you tomorrow."

"Thanks," Scott said.

He kept the pads on and hung the face mask on the handlebar of his bike as he and Kear rode home.

"Well, you're back in the saddle again," Kear said. "Feel better?"

"Yeah," Scott said.

But Lance Woodlawn came into his mind, spoiling some of the good thoughts about playing football again. He hated playing with anyone who had a grudge against him. And it had taken only a couple of plays to make Lance feel that way about him.

The thought led back to his duffel bag. Had he been framed by someone who had a grudge against him? Again, Peg came to mind. And Monk. But he could go crazy thinking about it. He didn't know if their grudges were serious enough, and he had no proof.

The minute he stepped into the kitchen with the shoulder pads and face mask, his mother confronted him. "Well, you needn't tell me what you've been up to."

"I'm going to play with the Cougars," Scott explained, plunking down onto a chair and dropping the face mask beside it.

"Oh, you are? And what do you think your father will think? He won't be happy about it. He wanted to ground you, you know."

"I know, Ma," Scott said. "But he didn't. And, like you said, isn't it enough that I got kicked off the Greyhawks, the team I *really* liked to play with?" Scott thought of another argument to convince his mother. "This is more than just a chance for me to play football."

"It is?" She looked skeptical.

"It's a chance for me to find out who framed me," he said, determined. "I'm going to prove I didn't put those joints in my duffel bag."

"And how do you plan to do that?" she wondered aloud.

Scott frowned. "I'm not sure. But I'll come up with something."

"I thought it was too late to sign up with another team, anyway," Mrs. Kramer said.

"The Cougars aren't in a league," Scott explained. "That's why I can join. They schedule games with anybody who's willing to play them."

He told her that he had to have another physical examination and that it would be paid for by the garage that sponsored the team.

"Did you tell this coach, who doesn't seem to have a name —"

"Coach Zacks," Scott said.

"Did you tell Coach Zacks that you *were* on a team before?"

"Yes, I told him."

"And why you're not on it now?"

Scott looked down at his feet. "No. He didn't ask, and I didn't tell him."

Mrs. Kramer took Scott's face in her hands. "Don't you think you've gotten into enough trouble already for not telling the truth, the whole truth, and nothing but the truth?"

"I guess," Scott admitted. "I'll tell him tomorrow, I promise." Then he added, "I mean, if it's okay with you and Dad that I play."

"Tell you what. If you keep your promise, I promise to go to your father on your behalf." She glanced at his clothes. "Now get out of those dirty things and take a shower," she said. "You smell worse than these onions I'm cooking."

He grinned, picked up his face mask, and headed for his room. It was great to have his mother on his side again. She won't regret it, he vowed to himself.

Shortly after three o'clock the next day, Scott had his physical and went home, part of a team once again.

But he had mixed feelings about it. Were the Cougars the team he really wanted to play with? Wouldn't he rather be with the Greyhawks?

He wasn't sure. If someone on the team had

framed him just to get him kicked off, he might rather play with the Cougars after all.

It felt odd going to practice alone that evening. The Greyhawks were practicing, too, and Kear had to be with them. As much as Scott missed his friend, though, he was more concerned about having to tell the coach why he was a player without a team.

The Cougars were already assembled at the park. Some of them were playing catch with a couple of footballs. Others were doing calisthenics.

Scott saw Coach Zacks standing by his station wagon. The coach motioned for him to come over.

"Heard some stuff about you," the coach said as Scott approached. "Not very good stuff."

Scott felt his face flush. So he wouldn't have to confess after all. Someone had beaten him to it.

"You smoke?" the coach asked.

"No."

"Some of my boys say you were caught smoking marijuana. That's why you're not playing football."

Scott's heart pounded. "I don't smoke," he insisted. "Somebody stuck a couple of joints in my duffel bag. My coach saw them when I opened up the bag. Would I have opened it up if I had known they were in there?"

"No, it doesn't seem that you would," Coach Zacks admitted. "Got any idea who put them in there?"

"Wish I did," said Scott.

He began fuming inside just thinking about it.

Coach Zacks cleared his throat. "I'm all for competition among my players," he said. "It keeps them on their toes. But it's bad news when stuff like that happens off the field." He lifted a uniform out of the station wagon and tossed it to Scott. "Here," he said. "You can put it on inside the car."

Scott crawled up into the station wagon, took off his pants and shirt, and put on the uniform. Then he put on the rubber-cleated shoes and helmet and joined the rest of the team.

Some of them greeted him by name. Others merely nodded to him. Lance Woodlawn, one of the guys playing catch, said "Hi."

"Hi," Scott said, surprised that Lance had addressed him. He'd been wondering how the tough tackle would react to him today after Monday's scrimmage.

Coach Zacks put the team through some grueling exercises first, snapping orders like an army sergeant. Then he split the team in two, team A playing defense, team B offense. He placed Scott on team B.

"Kramer, know what the play Forty-eight means?"

Scott nodded. "A back running through the eight hole," he said.

"Good boy," the coach said, patting him on the shoulder. "All right. Let's do it."

The sides lined up at the line of scrimmage. Zane Corbett shouted signals: "Down! Set! Hut! Hut! Hut!" The play was on. Before Scott had a chance to lunge toward Lance, he found himself triple-blocked! Not only did Lance rush at him, but so did the players on either side of him!

Scott found himself knocked back on his rear with the three players on top of him.

He caught Lance's smirk as Lance and the

other two players pushed themselves off him. Scott climbed slowly, achingly, to his feet and brushed off his pants.

"Four yards isn't bad, Barney," the coach said to the burly fullback who had carried the ball. "But you were a little slow. Let's try it again."

Oh, no, Scott thought.

This time, when the ball was snapped, he ducked low and tried to squeeze through the narrow gap between Lance and Jim Firpo, the left end who had joined Lance and the left guard to triple-block Scott on the first play.

He almost got through. But Lance grabbed his arm and held him long enough for Jim to lay a block against him.

Where's that whistle? Scott wondered, as he burst to his feet and stared at the coach.

"Did you see that, Coach?" he cried. "Lance grabbed my arm!"

"He did? Sorry, Kramer. I didn't see it. And if I didn't, a ref in a game might not have, either. Okay. Huddle!"

While the coach joined the defensive team in a huddle, Scott knelt in his position at the line of scrimmage. His body ached in the places where he'd been hit by the three guys on defense, and he began to wonder seriously if he'd made a mistake in joining the Cougars. They weren't only tough; they were mean. You'd think they were playing for money instead of for fun.

And it was obvious that Coach Zacks didn't care. As a matter of fact, it seemed that this was the kind of team he wanted.

The team practiced a full hour before the coach called it quits.

"We have a game against the Tigers on Wednesday at six o'clock," he announced. "It'll be at Taylor Field. Be there an hour before. If any of you can't make it, call me. You know the consequences if you don't. Okay. See you Wednesday."

Scott looked at Barney, the fullback. "What are the consequences if you don't call him?"

"Fifty push-ups," Barney said. He grinned. "Even if you called him, he might make you do forty. He's made me do it. You're a Cougar now, Scott. Better be there."

"Yeah. Right," Scott said.

He headed to the station wagon to get his

clothes and saw Jerilea Townsend and Fran Whitaker coming toward him. His stomach tightened. He hadn't spoken to Jerilea since the day he was kicked off the Greyhawks. She must have heard by now that the "cigarettes" were really pot.

"How'd you two know I was here?" he said, trying to keep his tone light.

"Kear told us," Jerilea said. "Anyway, I had to see you."

I knew it, Scott thought. She wants to tell me off.

"I spoke to Peg Moore. I pumped her, as a matter of fact," Jerilea went on.

"Huh?" Scott was confused.

"She says she didn't put the marijuana in your duffel. She *swears* she didn't. And I believe her."

"Wait a minute. So you know about the pot?" Scott asked.

"Yeah, everybody knows about it," Jerilea said. "You know how quickly rumors spread around school." Fran nodded in agreement.

"And you're not mad at me for not telling you?"

Jerilea brushed her hair from her eyes. "I was a little, at first. But then I figured you were just protecting yourself. Because of Eddie and all."

Scott winced slightly. Jerilea sure didn't mince words.

"Yeah, that's right," Scott said. "But I still don't get it. How come you asked Peg about it?"

Jerilea smiled. "Because I knew she liked you at one time. And I just wondered if she wanted to hurt you because you didn't feel the same way. You know, nothing like a woman scorned."

Scott's mouth dropped open, but no words came out. Jerilea did this for me? *Maybe she likes me more than I know.*

Some of the Cougars started whistling and making wisecracks at them. The girls looked in their direction and laughed.

"I've got to pick up my duds," he finally said. "Will you wait up?"

Scott retrieved his clothes and started home with the girls.

"So that leaves the mystery still unsolved," Jerilea said.

"Yeah," Scott said, the glum feeling returning. "Maybe it will *never* be solved."

They reached the intersection where they had to split up when Scott saw a familiar figure coming toward them.

"Hi, Jeri, Fran, Scott," Monk Robertson said as he got closer. "Boy, you're a good-looking trio. Even you in your fancy — what's that?" He leaned forward and stared at the name on the front of Scott's jersey. "Cougars?"

"That's right. Cougars," Scott said.

"Yeah. Heard you're playing with them," Monk said. "Too bad. We'll miss you, Scott."

"Somebody won't," Scott said.

Monk's gaze locked with his a moment. Then a grin spread across his face. "Well, got to go. See you guys later."

He waved as he walked past them. Scott glanced back at him for a second, thinking: that's a switch. Monk's usually a rat on the football field. Why does he suddenly come off acting like a nice guy?

Was it because of the girls being present? Or was it for some other reason?

Seven

Kear rode his bike over to Scott's house at about a quarter to five Wednesday afternoon, then the boys biked to Taylor Field. Scott wore his Cougars uniform and carried his shoes around his neck. Kear carried Scott's helmet in the basket on his handlebars.

"Don't let me forget to stop for some groceries after the game," Kear said. "My mom says that if I don't get any cereal tonight I won't have breakfast tomorrow."

"Don't you like eggs?" Scott asked.

"You kidding? Just the smell turns my stomach."

They arrived at the field and laid their bikes at the left side of the bleachers. Scott put on his shoes and helmet and began playing catch with Arnie Patch and Don Albright, two of the first team's running backs. Then Coach Zacks had the team do some running, jumping, and passing exercises until a few minutes before six, when the game started.

The Tigers won the toss and chose to receive.

Barney Stone kicked from the thirty-five yard line. A Tigers backfield man caught it on the Tigers' thirty-one and carried it to their thirty-nine, where Lance Woodlawn tackled him. Scott, trailing behind Lance, saw him push himself off the runner's back as if the runner were a log. He wished a referee had seen the unsportsmanlike conduct, but no whistle blew.

First and ten. The teams formed at the line of scrimmage.

"Hey! You're Kramer!" the tackle playing opposite Scott cried, loud enough for all twenty-two players — and the referee — to hear him. "Heard you were bounced off the Greyhawks, Kramer!"

Scott's heart jumped. He didn't say anything, afraid that it would only add fuel to the fire.

The Tigers' quarterback began barking signals.

"He was caught smoking grass," the guard next to the tackle said.

"I don't smoke — grass or anything else," Scott retorted.

The two players laughed. They're out to rile me, Scott thought. And they were succeeding.

"Hut three!" the quarterback called.

Angered by the two players' remarks, Scott lowered his head and plunged toward the gap between the left guard and left tackle. He felt himself being sandwiched in between the players as they tried to double-block him. Urging his body for extra effort, he managed to break through and dive at the running back, who had just taken a handoff from the quarterback.

The whistle shrilled.

A four-yard loss. The ball was put on the Tigers' thirty-five yard line. Second and fourteen.

"Hey! Got to watch this dog," the tackle said. "He's full of tricks."

"Yeah," the guard said, grinning.

Scott felt a light jab in his ribs. He glanced at Carl Trokowski next to him — who played center on offense — and received a wink.

On the next play, Scott and Carl double-blocked the Tigers' tackle. In a flash the Tigers' guard sprang on Carl, shoving him back hard enough to send the Cougars' guard sprawling to the ground. Scott and the Tigers' tackle stood shoulder-to-shoulder for a moment. Their gazes locked.

Suddenly a figure in orange and black rushed past Scott. Scott glanced at him, saw the football cached in the crook of his arm, and broke away from the tackle to go after him. He was too late. The runner went sixteen yards before Barney Stone brought him down.

The Tigers' tackle wore a smirk when he faced Scott on the line again. "It don't pay to use drugs, Kramer," he said sardonically. "It slows you down. Did you notice?"

"One thing I noticed is your big mouth," Scott said softly. "Even your face mask doesn't hide it."

The Tiger's grin vanished. He didn't answer.

They gained a yard on the next play, then lost possession of the ball on their twenty-eight when Carl managed to break through the line and sack the quarterback before he could hand the ball off to a running back.

Three plays later, with the Cougars on the Tigers' forty-eight yard line, Zane tossed a short pass over the scrimmage line intended for right end Mitch Bartell. But a tackle broke through, deflected the pass, and another Tiger caught it and raced down the sideline for a touchdown.

"Oh, no!" Scott moaned.

The tackle who had deflected the pass was the player Scott was supposed to block. Sammy Colt, he had heard some of the Tigers call him.

"Get with it, Kramer!" Lance Woodlawn snapped. "He's your man!"

They exchanged angry glances. Scott had to look away first; he knew it was his fault that Sammy had gotten past him.

The kick for the extra point was good, and the Tigers led, 7–0.

Three players from the Cougars bench ran onto the field replacing Scott and the linemen, Eddie Smits and Andy Tokarz.

Scott was glad for the break. He was hot and drenched with sweat. He took off his helmet and sat down.

He hadn't rested more than ten seconds when Coach Zacks came and stood before him. "Those Tigers' linemen getting to you, Scott?"

Scott shrugged. "No."

"You sure?"

Scott hesitated and shrugged again. "That Colt kid and the guard keep mentioning my getting caught smoking marijuana," he finally admitted. "I told them it wasn't true, but they keep nagging me about it."

"I figured it was that," said the coach. "Well, don't let them get your goat. Be tough. They're testing you, that's what they're doing."

Two minutes into the second quarter he sent Scott back into the game.

"Well, look who's back," Sammy Colt remarked, grinning that dirty grin of his. "Old Pothead Kramer."

Scott felt like belting him. "I told you," he said angrily. "I'm not into drugs! I never was! So get off my back!"

Sammy and the guard beside him exchanged

a smile. "You believe that, don't you, Tony?" he said.

"Sure I do," Tony said. "Like I believe in Santa Claus."

Smartmouths, Scott thought. Why did every team always seem to have at least one or two smartmouths?

The Cougars had the ball on their own forty-one. A run around right end by right halfback Don Albright got them across the fifty yard line to the Tigers' forty-nine.

First and ten.

"Nice run, Don," Zane said in the huddle. "Okay. Forty-eight. On your toes, Scott."

The team was ready to break out of the huddle when a sub came in. "Hold it," he said. "Trok, take off."

Carl broke out of the huddle and raced off the field.

"The coach says Fly Thirty-eight," the sub said.

Everybody stared at him. "A pass play? On a first down?"

A whistle shrilled.

"Delay of game," the ref snapped, running

forward and taking the ball from the sub who had just replaced Carl Trokowski. "Five-yard penalty."

"Oh, no," Zane Corbett moaned. "Now we *do* need something like a pass."

The ref placed the ball on the Cougars' forty-six yard line, trotted to the side, and blew his whistle again.

The Cougars scrambled to the line of scrimmage, where the Tigers were already waiting for them. Fly Thirty-eight, Scott reminded himself, was a pass from left halfback Arnie Patch to right end Mitch Bartell. They had worked on it a few times in practice.

"Down! Set! Hut! Hut! Hut!" Zane barked as he stood behind the substitute center, Bob Touse.

Bob centered the ball. Zane faded back, handed the ball off to Arnie, and Arnie started to fade to the left, his attention focused toward the far left side of the field to divert the Tigers' backfield.

Scott knew his job was to block Sammy Colt, then bolt past him and take out the middle linebacker. But he never got past Sammy.

Sammy had thrown himself down against Scott's legs, blocking Scott from going past him at all.

The play never got off. Arnie, not able to find Mitch free, hung on to the ball and was thrown for a fourteen-yard loss.

Once again the coach sent in a substitute for Scott.

"Scott," he said, looking intently into Scott's eyes. "I don't know what happened out there, but you sure fouled up the works. That play would've gone for a touchdown if you had stood on your feet and done your job."

Scott froze. He looked away and stared at the worn grass in front of him, his heart thumping. He had nothing to say. The coach was right. He hadn't done his job.

EIGHT

Five minutes before the half ended, Coach Zacks put Scott back into the game. The Tigers had racked up another touchdown while he'd been warming the bench. It was now Tigers 13, Cougars 0.

The ball was on the Tigers' thirty-three yard line, and it was the Tigers' ball. Scott saw that another kid was playing opposite him in Sammy Colt's place now.

Bill Fantry, the Tigers' quarterback, barked signals. Scott scrambled forward on the snap, bounced a shoulder off the Tigers' tackle, and tried to see the oncoming play. Fantry was fading back, looking for a receiver. But, from his right, the left halfback was racing toward him.

Scott, judging from the running back's move, headed toward Fantry's left side.

His judgment was perfect. The back took a handoff from Fantry and was heading toward his left side of the line when Scott smeared him.

A fumble!

Scott, seeing the ball bouncing deeper into Tigers territory, sprinted after it, picked it up, and raced all the way to the end zone!

Touchdown!

The Cougars' fans — what few there were — applauded and cheered.

"Great play, Scott!" Scott recognized Kear's voice. He turned and saw his friend sitting in the bleachers. Scott grinned and waved. Kear waved back.

Behind him sat a kid wearing a pith helmet and dark sunglasses. In front of him sat three other Greyhawks players: Monk Robertson, Elmo George, and Lenny Baccus. All three raised their fists in a salute to him and he smiled. He missed them. Even Monk, irascible as he was at times.

"I don't believe it," Lance Woodlawn said, as

the teams formed at the scrimmage line for the point-after play.

Scott grinned. "Well, believe it," he murmured.

Barney kicked the ball between the uprights. Tigers 13, Cougars 7.

The Tigers had the ball on the Cougars' twenty-two when the first half ended.

"Hey! You were on your toes on that play, Scott!" Coach Zacks said, as the teams trotted off the field, and he ran alongside Scott. "Good work!"

"Thanks," Scott said, carrying his helmet to let a cool breeze freshen his sweat-soaked head.

"Yeah! Nice play, Scott!" Carl Trokowski said, running up along the other side of Scott and breathing hard. Sweat beads were rolling down his cheeks. "Boy! Am I bushed!"

Scott grinned. Carl could lose twenty pounds and still be a big kid.

After a ten-minute intermission — which seemed like only ten seconds to Scott — the teams returned to the field for the start of the second half. Coach Zacks had delivered a short speech to the squad, directing most of his statements to a few of the players: "Jim, you went out after that pass telegraphing your move like a kid from Western Union. Don't keep waving your arms, okay? Arnie, on a handoff, put both arms over the ball. It's not a loaf of bread you're carrying. Scott, tackling that runner and then scooping up the ball and going for the touchdown was a great play. But you're not getting your head and shoulders down on the blocks. Hit your man solid, then make your next move, okay?"

The third quarter was only two minutes old when Zane released a long pass to Mitch Bartell from the Cougars' eighteen yard line. Bill Fantry, playing safety, leaped and practically took the ball out of Mitch's waiting hands on the thirty-eight. Hiding the ball under his left arm, he bolted down the left side of the field. Five yards . . . ten . . . fifteen . . .

Scott was the closest to him as Fantry started to reach the twenty. Scott dove at him, got a hand on him . . .

Fantry stiff-armed him, breaking loose Scott's

92

hold, and raced on down the field for a touch-down. Scott was sick.

"Hey! Don't look so sad!" Carl said to him, patting him on the head. "At least you got a hand on him! Nobody else was close!"

"I had him and lost him," Scott said, not wanting to meet any of the other players' eyes. Surely every one of them would show disgust.

Rod Holland, the Tigers' fullback, tried the point-after kick and missed it by inches. Tigers 19, Cougars 7.

The Tigers' fullback kicked off. The end-over-end kick was high and short and went directly to running back Don Albright. He caught the ball against his chest and raced up the field to the Cougars' forty-three, where he was tackled.

"Forty-eight," Zane said in the huddle.

Barney took the handoff from him, bolted up through the line behind Scott, and was thrown for a two-yard loss. Sammy Colt had faked Scott out and plunged through a hole to nab him before he could make a move. Nobody had to remind Scott of that. He knew it and blamed himself for it.

Nevertheless, in the huddle, Zane glared at him through his face mask. "Come on, Scott," he rasped. "Get on the stick. All right?"

"Maybe he can't," Lance said. "Maybe his brain has been damaged by you-know-what."

Scott bristled. Now Lance was acting just as bad as those two Tigers, referring to the rumor that Scott smoked pot.

Even so, Scott wondered if Lance wasn't right in a way. Maybe he couldn't play like the Cougars did: rough and dirty. Buck with your head . . . use your elbows . . . your fists . . . trip 'em up. Anything to get your man or gain as many yards as you can if you have the ball. That kind of football, Scott knew, had been drilled into their heads by their strong-willed coach, Joe Zacks.

I believe in winning, too, Scott thought. But I'm not here to break anybody's bones. I'm here to play clean, hard football. And to have fun. Mainly, to have fun. That's all. Say what you want to, Zane, Lance, and the rest of you guys, but that's the only way I'm going to play. And if Coach Zacks doesn't like it and wants to boot me off the team, let him. I've been a player

94

without a team before. I can be a player without a team again.

"Weirdo Fourteen," Zane said. "On two!"

Scott stared at him. "Weirdo Fourteen?"

"What's the matter? Haven't you heard of that play before? Let's go!"

"No! What is it?" Scott said, as the team broke out of the huddle.

"You'll see," Zane said. "Just do your job. Stop Colt and Moss."

Scott glared at him as the ends, guards, and tackles formed at the line of scrimmage. They were pulling a play that he had never heard of. Why were they doing this? To offend him? To show him how tough they were? How high and mighty?

He glanced at Lance Woodlawn crouched beside him, right hand braced against the turf. Lance's attention was directed straight ahead. Serious determination showed on his face.

"What's the play?" Scott asked him.

"Weirdo Fourteen. You heard him," Lance said, not looking at him.

Zane barked signals. The ball was snapped on the second "Hut!" and Scott bolted forward.

Like a cue ball, he bounced his left shoulder against Sammy Colt's left, then his right shoulder off Tony Moss's right. At the same time, he looked beyond the line of scrimmage at the Tigers' backfield defense and saw the two safeties running toward the right corner. A second later a green uniform came into his line of vision, and he recognized the short, husky figure of Barney Stone sprinting down the field.

He realized then that Weirdo Fourteen was nothing but a pass play from the quarterback to the fullback. Why didn't Zane just say so?

Scott saw the ball land in Barney's hands just as somebody struck him from behind, sending him sprawling to the ground. A flag went down.

Scott leaped to his feet, whirled around, and saw Sammy Colt standing before him, looking hard at him.

"What was that for?" Scott demanded.

"My mistake," Sammy replied.

"That mistake cost you fifteen yards," the referee snapped.

Sammy stared at him. "For what?"

"Clipping, that's what," the referee answered glibly.

The pass had netted the Cougars twenty-one yards. They had the choice of accepting that or the fifteen-yard penalty. He must be kidding, Scott thought, but the ref was quite serious when he asked Zane to decide.

"We'll take the gain," Zane answered just as seriously. He glanced at Scott and grinned. "Now you know what Weirdo Fourteen is, right?"

"Yeah," said Scott. He didn't appreciate Zane's teasing. But he didn't want to make matters worse, either, by talking back to him.

First and ten. Cougars' ball on the Tigers' thirty-eight yard line.

"Line buck," Zane said in the huddle. "Forty-eight, on three. Let's go!"

They broke out of the huddle, lined up on the scrimmage line, and Zane shouted signals. On the third "Hut!" Carl snapped the ball. Scott and the other linemen proceeded to do their jobs as Barney broke from his position behind right tackle and took the handoff from Zane.

The play failed. No one had counted on the Tigers' strategy, a seven-man Red Dog. Two ends, the two tackles, and three backfield men charged through the line in a burst of strength and speed that not only surprised the Cougars, but also resulted in Barney's getting tackled the instant he had the ball. It was a three-yard loss.

In the huddle, Zane glared at one lineman and then another. "What happened to you guys?" he snarled, loud enough for the Tigers to hear him. "They went through you like an armored truck!"

"They Red-Dogged us," Carl complained.

"I know what they did!" Zane snorted. "But you guys let 'em!" He paused as he looked from one lineman to another again. "Okay. We've got three downs to make thirteen yards. Let's try another pass. You ends, keep your eyes peeled. It'll be to one of you. And, look, you tackles and guards: do your jobs, okay? If you haven't got the guts, say so. Zacks doesn't want gutless guys." He stared at Scott as he said it. "Okay! On two!" he finished, and the huddle broke.

Scott's temper flared up for a moment. He was sure now he was on no ordinary football team. These guys were out to win. No matter how.

NINE

Scott made sure he did a good job of blocking Sammy Colt, then gave him a hard, final shove before turning to block Al Johnson, the other tackle.

Suddenly Scott saw J. J. Whipple, the Tigers' center — who played middle linebacker on defense — plunging toward the center of the line. Knowing that J. J. would get past the scrimmage line unless he was stopped, Scott pushed Al aside and started after him, exerting all of his energy to get to the would-be tackler before it was too late.

At the last moment, Scott dove in front of J. J., stopping the linebacker cold with a solid block.

Then, not more than five feet beyond him, Scott saw Zane rear back and heave a pass toward the left side of the field. He rolled over on his side and looked behind him. A feeling of exaltation filled him as he saw the ball spiraling toward Jim Firpo's outstretched hands. Then Jim had it, and he ran on into the end zone for a touchdown.

Tigers 19, Cougars 13.

"Nice block, Scott!" a voice yelled from the bleachers.

Scott recognized it as Kear's, turned, and lifted his hand briefly in a wave to his friend. Kear was alone now. Even the kid in the pith helmet and sunglasses was gone.

"Guess it pays to jump on you jokers once in a while," Zane quipped. "Good blocking, you guys."

None of the tackles or guards, including Scott, acted as though they'd heard him.

"You, too, Kramer," Zane added. "You got that guy just in time, or I might not have gotten off that pass."

So he doesn't mind showering a little praise on a guy once in a while, Scott thought.

"I was lucky," Scott said finally.

"Lucky, heck. You did what you had to do," Zane replied.

Talks like a coach, Scott thought.

Barney successfully kicked the ball between the uprights for the point-after. Tigers 19, Cougars 14. The Cougars still needed a touchdown to forge ahead of the Tigers.

They didn't get it. The game ended with the Tigers winning, 19–14.

"We should've taken those guys," Scott heard Coach Zacks say as the coach ran off the field between Zane and Lance. "If we hadn't pulled some boners, we would have."

He sounded more angry than disappointed, Scott thought, running a few feet behind them. The uniforms of both players were spotted with dirt and grime. Yet they still weren't half as dirty as his own or the other players', Scott saw. Which meant one thing: they had played a tough game.

No, it was more than a game; it was a battle.

I've never played so hard in my life, Scott thought. And I don't remember ever being so tired in my life. That wasn't fun. That was work.

Coach Zacks's chief concern was to win, and he was mad if he didn't.

Sportsmanship didn't seem to be in his vocabulary, Scott told himself. How long could I play on a team like this?

Right now, he didn't know. He just knew that today's game was no fun. Even if the Cougars had won it, it still would not have been fun.

That was the difference in playing with the Greyhawks, he reflected. Aside from that smartmouth Monk Robertson, the guys were great fun to play with. And Coach Dresso was a fine man. Sure he played to win, but it wasn't top priority with him. He believed in playing football for fun, too. He never risked the health and physical pains of his players just for a touchdown. He was fair, probably the fairest coach in the league.

And strict when it came to rules. Otherwise, wouldn't he have believed me, Scott thought, and kept me on the team? Or did he boot me off not because he didn't believe me, but because the odds were against me?

Whatever the case, Scott liked and respected Coach Dresso. He wished he could exonerate himself somehow and get back with the Greyhawks. But how could he? Right now he couldn't see a chance of *ever* getting back with them.

He saw Kear running toward him from the bleachers and waited for him.

"Hi!" Kear said, slowing down as he got closer. "Some game."

"Yeah," Scott agreed. "Sure was."

They headed toward the gate.

"I just remembered I've got to get groceries," Kear said.

"Yeah," said Scott. "Hope you didn't forget your wallet like you did that one time we both had to go."

"I made sure before I —" Kear started to say, reaching into his back pocket. Then he shouted, "Hey! It's gone! My wallet's gone!"

TEN

"Maybe it dropped out of your pocket while you were sitting in the bleachers," Scott guessed.

"I don't know," Kear said. His eyes were wide with worry. "I'll go back and look."

"I'll get my stuff," Scott said.

While Kear raced back to the bleachers, Scott went into the clubhouse and picked up his duffel bag. Then he ran back outside and down the field toward the bleachers, where he saw Kear searching the seats.

"No luck yet?" Scott shouted.

"No!" Kear answered, leaning forward and peering down between the seats at the ground below.

Then he ran to the edge of the bleachers,

jumped down, and checked underneath where he'd been sitting. Scott followed him and began helping him in the search.

The wallet was nowhere to be seen.

"I had five bucks in it for the groceries I had to buy," Kear said, his voice sounding anxious.

"Think you lost it before you came into the park?" Scott asked him.

"No. I'm sure I —" Kear paused. He suddenly focused on Scott's duffel bag. "Scott —" he began and faltered.

Scott looked at his bag. When he saw that it was partially unzipped, his eyes widened. He definitely remembered zipping it up after putting his towel and soap in it.

An eerie sensation crept over him as he saw something brown and shiny inside it. He didn't need any further examination to know what it was.

Unzipping the bag a few more inches, he extracted a leather wallet.

"It's mine," Kear said, his voice faint.

His hand shaking, Scott handed it to him. "I can't believe this," he declared, incredulous. "How'd it get in there?"

Kear looked at him. "I don't know."

"Oh, no," Scott moaned, staring at the accusing expression on Kear's face. "You don't think *I* stole it from you? Why would I —?" He couldn't finish. The look in Kear's eyes and on his face suggested that Kear didn't know whether to believe him or not.

Kear looked inside the wallet. A groan escaped his lips. "It's gone," he said, his face turning white. "The money's gone."

He folded the wallet, stuffed it into his rear pocket, and stormed off.

"Kear!" Scott cried, running after him. "I didn't take it! I *swear* I didn't! Look! You don't think I could've taken it while I was in a game, do you?"

"I don't know what to think!" Kear exclaimed, running faster toward the gate.

"I didn't take your wallet, Kear!" Scott repeated, his heart aching. "Believe me! For crying out loud, you're my best friend! Why would I do a lousy thing like that?"

Kear didn't answer. He ran out of the gate and down the street, leaving Scott staring after him.

I can't believe this! Scott thought, choking back tears. I just can't! Somebody must have taken Kear's wallet, lifted the money, then put the wallet in my duffel bag.

Who'd do a dirty, double-crossing thing like that?

Suddenly he thought: I know who. The same person who had put the two marijuana cigarettes in it. That's who.

Sadly, he walked home alone. He had been framed again, this time resulting in the loss of his best and closest friend.

What kind of a person would do this to him? Who could hate him so much to hurt him like that?

He went over and over all the guys he knew, including the Greyhawks players who'd been sitting in front of Kear at the game; Monk Robertson, Elmo George, Lenny Baccus. But none of them seemed capable of pulling off not just one, but two mean, dirty tricks on him. Not one.

He tried to avoid his parents' eyes as he entered the house and trudged through the kitchen, heading to his room.

"From the looks of your face and your uniform, I'd say you lost a tough battle," his father observed, gazing at him over the evening paper. He was sitting at the kitchen table. "What was the score?"

"We lost — nineteen to fourteen," Scott replied.

"Not bad," his father said. "Not bad enough to match that expression on your face, anyway."

Scott didn't answer him. He had to cool off awhile before saying anything about Kear's wallet — if he mentioned it at all.

He got to his room, dropped the duffel bag on the floor, stripped out of his uniform, and took a shower. Usually a good shower not only made him feel cleaner, but it made him feel better, too.

Not this time. This time he felt just as bad after the shower as he did before it. He couldn't wash the wallet-in-his-duffel-bag incident out of his mind.

He still felt lousy at the supper table.

"Something's bothering you. You haven't

looked this bad since you were booted off the Greyhawks," his father observed, scooping up some scalloped potatoes. "Come on. What is it this time?"

"It . . ." Scott cleared his throat. He had tried to hide his feelings. Obviously he had failed.

He told them about the wallet. "Guess I'd better get rid of that duffel bag," he said when he finished.

"No, you don't," his mother said, her voice firm. "Somebody's out to frame you for some reason or other. Why? That's the question."

"Or maybe he's lying again," his father cut in quietly, but sharply. "Maybe he stole the money to buy more pot."

Scott stared at him. His face went white. "No! That's not true! I would never steal from Kear! Nor from anybody else!"

He looked at his mother. "I swear it, Ma. I didn't steal Kear's wallet."

She looked from him to her husband. "Ed," she said gently, "just because Eddie smoked pot in high school doesn't mean that Scott would do it, too."

"Maybe not," Mr. Kramer said. "But don't

you think it's quite a coincidence that grass was found in Scott's duffel bag, and then his best friend's wallet is stolen?"

Scott's heart pounded so hard it felt as if it were going to jump out of his chest. Angered that his father could misjudge him so, he got up from the table and headed straight for his room. There are times, he thought, when Dad doesn't seem to know who I am. This was one of those times.

He lay on the bed, his hands behind his head, and thought of Eddie. Two years had passed since Eddie had been caught smoking marijuana. It seemed that everyone in Marlowe had heard about it. It was one of the most distressing periods of his family's life.

He couldn't let them go through that again. Somehow, he had to get to the bottom of this terrible thing. He had to prove to his father, and to everybody else, that he was innocent. He had to find the culprit.

He thought about calling Eddie. Eddie had gone through the real thing before and would know how he felt. Right now he needed somebody like Eddie to talk to, and Eddie would appreciate it.

He phoned Eddie later that night. He hadn't talked with his brother in two or three weeks — not since the last time his mother and father had called him.

"Eddie? Hi. This is Scott," he said when he had Eddie on the line. "How're you doing?"

"Fine. Hey, this is a nice surprise. What's up?"

Scott told him. It was hard at first, but once he got going, he was able to tell his brother everything.

"The thief had to be somebody at the game," Eddie assumed. "Anybody there you knew?"

"Besides Kear? Yeah. Monk Robertson, Elmo George, and Lenny Baccus. They all play for the Greyhawks."

"I know them," Eddie said. "Who's taking your place on the Greyhawks?"

"Sid Seaver," Scott answered.

"*Sid* Seaver? Rick's brother?"

"Yeah."

"Their father used to play semi-pro foot-

111

ball," Eddie said. "I remember watching him when I was a kid. As a matter of fact, Rich — that was his name, Rich — had a brother who used to play, too. They were on the same team and were called the Seaver Double Threat because they were so good."

"I didn't know that," Scott said.

"Then the brother joined the Peace Corps in Africa," Eddie went on. "I remember seeing him once after he got out. He was loaded down with African mementos."

"Where is he now?" Scott asked.

"I don't know. Maybe Dad can tell you," Eddie said.

Maybe he could, Scott thought. But he wasn't about to ask him now. It would have to wait until this dirty mess was cleaned up and over with.

But this story about the Seavers definitely sparked Scott's interest. Maybe Rick was the one behind it all, because he wanted history to repeat itself.

He thanked Eddie for all his help, and then hung up and dialed Kear Nguyen's number. Kear would certainly be interested in this tidbit.

Mrs. Nguyen answered.

"This is Scott Kramer," Scott said. "Can I talk with Kear, please?"

"Of course," she said. "Just a minute."

A few seconds later Kear was on the phone. "Yes?"

"Kear," Scott said, tense, "I've got to talk to you."

"I don't think I want to talk to you," Kear replied. "Ever again."

ELEVEN

Shortly after two o'clock the next afternoon, Scott was sitting in a booth in Dan's Yogurt Shoppe having yogurt with Jerilea Townsend. The temperature was cool, but a waffle cone of chocolate yogurt tasted good this time of day. And he'd had enough money to pay for Jerilea's, too.

"I have a sneaking suspicion of who's framed me," he said softly, looking across the table at her. "But I can't say or do anything until I have proof."

Her fingers tightened on her purse. "Who?"

"I told you. I can't say."

Jerilea shrugged and took a bite of her yogurt. "Okay. Your prerogative." *Prerogative.*

114

She'll probably be an English teacher when she grows up, Scott thought.

"I did want to talk to Kear Nguyen about it, though," he confessed.

"And?"

"He hung up on me."

"Really? Why?"

Scott explained about Kear's wallet being found in his duffel bag, without the five dollars in it.

"And he thinks *you* took it?" Jerilea exclaimed.

"Shhh!" Scott said, waving at her. "For crying out loud, I don't want the whole city to know about this!"

"I'm sorry," she whispered, her large eyes glancing around the room before settling back on his. "But it's terrible! You're his best friend!"

"It makes no difference. He still thinks I stole his money."

"Ignorance," Jerilea snorted. "Just plain ignorance." Then she jumped slightly in her seat. "Oh, I almost forgot about this." She opened her purse and took out a tiny tape recorder.

"Was that on the whole time?" Scott asked, dumbfounded.

She nodded. "Listen," she said, flicking a button on the machine. There was a whirring sound, then a click. A voice began to speak: "I don't know about you, but I'd take yogurt over ice cream any day."

"You would? Nah! I'd like a change."

Scott laughed. That was Jerilea and he talking. Then he heard their conversation about Kear's wallet, and he grew sober. He reached over to press the off button.

"What were you trying to do, get a confession out of me?"

"Of course not," Jerilea insisted. "I'm just fooling around with this thing. It used to be my dad's. He gave it to me after he decided he needed a more sophisticated model."

"He's a neurosurgeon, isn't he?"

"Yeah," she said. "Anytime you need a brain transplant, I'm sure he'd oblige."

"I'll remember that." Scott laughed.

Her gaze darted past him as he heard the yogurt shop's door open and close. The change

of expression on her face suggested that she recognized someone.

"Guess who just walked in," she said.

He frowned. "Kear?"

"No. Monk and Elmo."

She smiled and waved to them. Moving slowly, she picked up the tape recorder and pushed it into her small white purse.

"Well, hi, guys!" Monk greeted them as he stopped by their booth. "Filling up on yogy, I see. Hey," he went on, slapping Scott on the back, "those Cougars are really gung ho. You should've won."

Scott shrugged. "We should've. But we didn't."

"You played a good game, though, Scott," Elmo broke in. "I hope your coach noticed that."

Scott shrugged again. He hoped so, too.

His mind quickly reverted to his latest problem.

"Hey, guys," he said, "did any of you see anybody near my duffel bag the day I found those marijuana cigarettes in it?"

"I don't hang around the locker room any longer than I have to," Monk said gruffly.

"But did you see anybody —?"

"No," Monk cut him off short. "I didn't see anybody near your duffel bag. You should have a lock on it, anyway. You can't trust anybody these days."

"I do what I have to do and get out of there," Elmo replied. "If there was anybody near your duffel bag, I wouldn't know."

"How about the kid in a pith helmet and sunglasses sitting behind Kear Nguyen at the game?" Scott asked. "Know who he was?"

"Sure. Rick Seaver," Monk said. "Hey, man, what is this? The third degree?" He tapped Elmo's arm and started to head down the aisle. "Let's go. I'm thirsty. See you guys."

"Yeah," Scott said.

After the boys were gone, Scott looked at Jerilea and said absently, "Rick. Rick and Sid. It adds up."

Jerilea's eyes widened. "You think Rick stole Kear's wallet?"

"He could have. He was sitting behind Kear, and a guy could get so wrapped up in a game he'd never know somebody was picking his pocket." He watched her remove the tape recorder from her purse. "You had it on?"

She nodded, smiling, and pressed a button. There was a whirring sound as the tape rewound. Then she pressed another button, and a moment later they heard the conversation among Monk, Elmo, and Scott.

"He's so arrogant I wouldn't be surprised if he had pulled off that dirty trick himself," Jerilea said caustically.

Scott shrugged. "Monk? Maybe. But why would he do it? I've never done anything to him."

"But you've never done anything to *anybody*, Scott," Jerilea said, reaching out and taking his hand. "You're considerate. A lot of kids aren't." She smiled. "That's why I like you."

"Hey, I'm no saint."

"No. But you're far from being a devil."

"I wish more people felt that way about me. Like my father," Scott said with a sigh. Then he squeezed her hand. "I've been thinking."

"I thought I smelled rubber burning." She laughed.

"I'm going to ask Coach Zacks if he can schedule a practice game with the Greyhawks."

"Why?"

"You've given me an idea," Scott replied. "Could I borrow your tape recorder for a few days?"

"Oh, I think I know what you're up to. You can keep it for as long as you need to."

He grinned. "Thanks, Jeri."

They wadded up their napkins, dumped them into the trash container, then waved to Monk and Elmo as they headed for the door.

"I'll walk you home, then get my bike and ride over to Coach Zacks's house," Scott said.

"Okay."

It was about twenty minutes later when Scott pulled up into Coach Zacks's driveway on Cornwall Lane. He set his bike up on the stand and went up the front porch steps to the white-paneled door. He knocked, and a few seconds later a tall, dark-haired woman with glasses answered.

"Hi. I'm Scott Kramer," Scott said. "I'm one of Coach Zacks's football players. Is he in?"

She looked at him a moment before she said, "Yes, he is. Just a minute."

She left, and in a moment the coach appeared. "Hi, Scott," he greeted. "Come on in."

Coach Zacks led him into a spacious living room.

"Sit down, Scott," Coach Zacks said, easing himself into an armchair. "What can I do for you?"

"I just wondered if we ah . . . if we can get a practice game with the Greyhawks," Scott said, feeling a trifle nervous.

Coach Zacks smiled. "The team you used to play on? That's an idea. As a matter of fact, it's a *good* idea. Why? You have any special reason why you'd like to play against them?"

Scott shrugged. "Yeah. A very special reason," he answered and took a deep breath. "I just can't tell you what it is right now," he added quietly.

TWELVE

At Tuesday's practice session, Coach Zacks informed the Cougars that they would be playing the Greyhawks the next day. Not even Scott knew before then that a game had definitely been arranged.

Scott had felt nervous about it ever since he had talked with Coach Zacks. Now that the game was ready to be played, he felt more nervous than ever. He was glad Coach Zacks hadn't pressed him into explaining why he'd like the Cougars to play against his former team. That was a secret he couldn't tell anyone. Not until the right moment came, anyway — and he hoped it would be sometime during the game.

Kickoff time was six o'clock. The Cougars won the toss and chose to receive.

Monk Robertson kicked off at the thirty-five, a low, shallow kick that went for thirty yards. Arnie Patch caught it and advanced it to the Cougars' forty-four, where Bill Lowry brought him down.

"Hey! You finally did it!" Scott heard Monk yell at Bill.

Bill looked at him not too pleasantly. "What do you mean . . . I finally did it?"

"Made the first tackle!" Monk exclaimed, running over and slapping Bill on the back. "Congratulations!"

Scott grinned. Not every guy on the team received such sparkling accolades from the Greyhawks' arrogant fullback.

He saw Kear slap Bill on the hip, and, for a moment, Kear's and Scott's eyes met. His mouth opened to say "Hi, Kear," but Kear looked away before he could. After a few seconds Kear trotted off to join the rest of the Greyhawks.

Scott had a feeling he couldn't explain. He had never played against his own team before — or what had once been his team. And, even though Kear was sore at him, playing against him didn't seem right.

Somehow I'm going to make him realize I'm not the stinker he thinks I am, Scott promised himself. And with luck I will today.

"Huddle!" Zane Corbett barked.

The Cougars quickly gathered.

"Forty-six . . . on three!" Zane said.

They broke out of the huddle and formed on the line of scrimmage. Scott's heart began to pound the instant he was face-to-face with Sid Seaver. He expected to see some evidence — some telltale sign — in those dark eyes that would reveal Sid's guilty conscience. But Sid returned his look as if nothing else was on his mind except the matter at hand: the football game.

I'll wait until I find the chance to get close to Rick, Scott thought. It's Rick I want, anyway. He's the one who framed me. For all I know Sid might be innocent of the whole thing. He's the quiet one of the two. Rick might not even have told him about framing me. He probably didn't trust Sid to keep quiet, even though Sid was the reason behind it all. Only Rick had the guts to think up that Seaver Double Threat idea.

"Down! Set! Hut! Hut! Hut!"

Carl snapped the ball. Zane grabbed it, pedaled back a few steps, then handed it off to Barney. Barney broke through tackle, sprinting at Scott's heels as Scott bumped the Greyhawks' tackle and guard — his old teammates Roy Austin and Chuck Bellini — in an attempt to wedge a hole between them.

It was a good run. Barney got the ball to the Cougars' forty-eight.

Second and six.

Barney carried again. But this time he fumbled the ball on the Cougars' forty-nine, and the Greyhawks recovered it.

"Oh, no!" Zane moaned.

Barney was angry, too. Scott could read the disgusted look on his face. There was one consolation from the loss of the ball: the opportunity to get face-to-face with Rick Seaver.

He got his chance on the second down, after

he broke through the line and tackled Rick for a two-yard loss.

"Hi, ol' buddy," Scott said, grinning. "Stuck any grass into somebody's duffel bag lately?"

Rick stared at him. "What're you talking about? You nuts?"

"You only wear your sunglasses and your uncle's pith helmet when you're a spectator at football games?"

"Are you crazy? You've lost your buttons, you know that?"

"I don't think so," Scott said, his smile faded.

"Huddle!" Rick shouted to his men.

Scott turned his back to him, feeling better now that he had broken the ice. But Rick was a tough nut to crack. What else could I say that would break him? he wondered. How could I get Rick to confess that he had framed me? That was the big job now.

In four plays the Greyhawks got the ball to the Cougars' four yard line, and each time Scott had the opportunity to be face-to-face with Rick, he repeated his innuendos but with variations: "Come on, Rick. You know what I'm talking about. You know who put those joints in my duffel bag. And you know —"

"I *don't* know!" Rick shouted, staring at him hotly. "Now stop saying that! Is that why we're playing this game? So that you can get at me?"

Scott matched his stare. "I could've phoned. But I figured you would hang up on me. This is the best and easiest way."

"The best and easiest way, is it? I don't believe you, you know that?" Rick said, boiling mad. "No matter what I say —"

"That's right," Scott cut in. "No matter what you say, because I know you're the one."

Rick's fists were clenched. His eyes were like steel.

"Go ahead, hit me," Scott said. "That would really prove it, wouldn't it?"

The Cougars' defense held like a brick wall in every way it could, short of causing heavy penalties. As usual, the guys played rough. Seeing the two teams together confirmed Scott's belief that, despite what had happened, he was still a Greyhawk at heart. Sure, a few of his old teammates got rough at times, too, but they always played fair and for fun.

The whistle shrilled with the ball on the one yard line.

"First down!" the ref shouted. "Cougars' ball!"

The Cougars tried an end-around run that went for eleven yards. On another try Don Albright carried again but fumbled. Kear Nguyen scooped it up and sprinted into the end zone for a touchdown.

For a moment Scott caught Kear's eye, flashed a hint of a smile, and pumped his fist. No matter what he thinks of me, I'm still his friend, Scott thought. I'm glad he made the touchdown.

Monk tried the point-after kick and put it straight between the uprights. Greyhawks 7, Cougars 0.

Before the half was over, the Greyhawks scored again on a pass from Rick to tight end Karl Draper. But this time Monk's kick missed the uprights by three feet. Greyhawks 13, Cougars 0.

It seemed, Scott thought, that Coach Zacks's

hope of beating the pants off the Greyhawks wasn't going to come true today. There was still plenty of time, though, for the Cougars to make a comeback.

During intermission, Scott couldn't think about anything except for his brief encounters with Rick Seaver during the first half. It bothered him that he still had no definite proof. What good was it to continually harass Rick if no one had witnessed the crimes — for crimes they were — or if Rick didn't confess to them? No good at all.

The second half started off with a bang. Barney Stone kicked off for the Cougars and managed to unleash one of his longest kicks. It sailed to the Greyhawks' twelve yard line, where Elmo George caught it and carried it back to their nineteen before Scott tackled him.

Scott wasn't sure how to judge the expression on Elmo's face as he put out his hand and helped Elmo to his feet. "Surprised?" he said. "Remember, I'm a Cougar right now."

Elmo grinned. "Yeah. I can see that," he said.

The Greyhawks tried two running plays, totaling seven yards, then Rick pedaled back and unleashed a long pass intended for split end Karl Draper.

Karl was about to catch it, when Arnie Patch, the Cougars' lightning-footed running back, snatched it from his grasp and bolted down the sideline for a touchdown. It was a sixty-eight-yard run, and the Cougars' fans applauded like crazy.

Barney booted the ball between the uprights for the extra point. Greyhawks 13, Cougars 7.

It wasn't until three minutes before the third quarter ended that Scott found himself staring down into Rick Seaver's face. Rick's helmet had been knocked off when Scott tackled him for a six-yard loss on the Cougars' thirty-eight yard line, and now Rick was down on the ground with Scott on top of him.

"What did you do with the money you found in Kear's wallet, Rick?" he whispered harshly. "Spend it on yourself and your girlfriend?"

"Sure. He took her out to dinner, didn't you, Rick?"

The voice came from Bill Lowry, who had fallen on his knees next to Scott and Rick and was slowly rising to his feet.

131

"Yeah, sure," Rick said. "I bought a big dinner for us. Now will you get off my —?"

"A big dinner for five bucks?" Bill Lowry cut in. "Oh, yeah! Maybe at McDonald's! Or Burger King!"

He chuckled as he rose to his feet, shoved Scott aside, and extended a hand to Rick. "You heard him, Scott. Get off his back."

Scott, rolling off Rick, looked up into the sweating, masked face of the Greyhawks' big right guard. His mind was churning rapidly, dredging up all the facts he could remember about his two frame-ups. From the corner of his eye he saw Rick rise to his feet and walk away, casting a cold, hard glance back at him, muttering something Scott couldn't hear.

"Wait a minute, Bill," Scott said, as the burly guard started away, too. "How did you know there was five dollars in Kear's wallet?"

Bill's eyes widened. Then he laughed. "Who doesn't know it? Everybody knows it."

"No, Bill," Scott said. "Nobody knows it except three people. Four, counting Kear's mother. Kear, me, and the person who had stolen his wallet."

"Baloney!" Bill snorted and started to walk away.

Scott grabbed his arm, just as the whistle shrilled for the start of the next play. "No. It's no baloney, Bill," Scott said. "You took that wallet from Kear while he was watching the Cougars-Tigers game, didn't you? Then you took the five-dollar bill out of it, went to the clubhouse, and put the wallet in my duffel bag."

"You can't prove nothing," Bill snapped, yanking his arm loose and starting to walk away again.

Again Scott caught his arm. "It was you, then, who put the joints in my duffel bag. Why, Bill? For Pete's sake, what did I ever do to you? Why did you frame me so that I'd be kicked off the team?"

Bill looked around furtively as if he wanted to make sure no one else was within listening range. "Because I got fed up being made a fool of all the time, that's why!" he exclaimed. "No matter what I did, I got bawled out. More than anybody else. Did the coach care that I was trying my best? No! He just kept bugging me . . . reminding me to get on the stick. Know

how many times he's said that to me? A hundred and one times! Well, I got sick of it."

"So you picked me as the scapegoat."

"Yeah. I guess I was jealous. You've been going big guns, and me . . ." He shrugged. "I'm just a dumb guard."

"Then, to make matters worse, you stole Kear's wallet," Scott said. "You *knew* he'd blame me for it, didn't you?"

"Yeah. I was sitting there, and I saw it sticking out of his pocket," Bill said, his voice almost a whisper. "It was an easy steal. I figured you'd be blamed because you'd want dough to buy more joints."

"Thanks, Bill," Scott said, trying to keep himself from punching the big tackle in the mouth. "Thanks a bunch. I like you, too."

"Bill!" a voice shouted. "Get your tail over here, will you?"

The whistle shrilled again.

"Five yards!" the ref shouted, pointing at the Greyhawks. "Delay of game!"

"Your fault, Bill!" somebody snapped angrily.

Bill shot a pale glance at Scott. "Too bad you

don't have proof," he said. He turned and headed toward the line of scrimmage, where the referee had marked off five yards against the Greyhawks.

Scott smiled. "Ah . . . but I do, Bill," he said. "I do."

THIRTEEN

The game ended with the Greyhawks regaining possession of the ball on their own two yard line. Even after a short pass that went awry, and three line plunges, the Cougars couldn't score, and the game went to the Greyhawks, 13–7.

"Getcha next time," Lance Woodlawn said to the Greyhawks team in general, as both clubs walked off the field.

"Sure you will," Monk Robertson answered, smiling.

Scott didn't care one way or another. He had hoped that the game would be a way to solve his problem, and it had. He had found out what he wanted to know: who had framed him. Maybe the next time both teams met, winning or losing would mean something. But not this time.

He waited outside the clubhouse for the members of the Greyhawks to leave. Almost always Coach Tom Dresso was the last one to depart, making sure that nobody left anything behind, that the place was cleaned up, the lights turned off, and the door locked.

"Coach!" Scott called to him, as he saw the coach step out and start locking the door.

Coach Dresso turned his head. "Oh. Scott Kramer. So you've found a team who would take you on. Well, I guess their coach isn't as strict as the coaches in our league."

Scott stepped up to him, holding out a hand-sized tape recorder. "I'd like you to listen to this, Coach," he said.

Coach Dresso frowned. He took the recorder, examined it a bit, then flicked a switch. After a few seconds voices began to speak. They were slightly muffled, but clear enough to identify the speakers and what they were saying. The coach's frown deepened.

"What is this?" he asked.

"That's Rick Seaver and me talking during the game," Scott said. "Keep listening."

There were sounds of grunts and groans and leather against leather, which the recorder had picked up before Scott had turned it off. He didn't want all that garbage on tape, but sometimes he hadn't been able to turn it off in time.

Suddenly it came to the part where his voice said, "What did you do with the money you found in Kear's wallet, Rick? Spend it on yourself and your girlfriend?"

Scott watched the coach's expression as a new voice chimed in. "Sure. He took her out to dinner, didn't you, Rick?"

The coach looked at Scott. "That Bill Lowry?"

Scott nodded.

"Yeah, sure," Rick's voice came from the tape. "I bought a big dinner for us. Now will you get off my —"

And then the beginning of the end for Bill Lowry: "A big dinner for five bucks? Oh, yeah! Maybe at McDonald's! Or Burger King!"

The coach listened to it all, and when the tape ended he stared at Scott, dumbfounded.

139

"Well, I'll be darned!" he said. "You did all this by yourself? This . . . this detective work?"

Scott shrugged. "Well, the tape recorder belongs to Jerilea Townsend. I borrowed it from her, and my mom sewed a pocket inside my jersey so I could get at it easily. I was afraid, at first, that it might get crushed if I was hit by somebody. But it's okay. Anyway, it was the only way I could prove I was innocent. The funny part of it is, I thought it was Rick Seaver who was framing me. I was sure it was him for a couple of reasons — until Bill Lowry spoke up."

"Guess he cooked his own goose, didn't he?" the coach said, shaking his head sadly.

Scott nodded. "He sure did. At the same time, he got me off the hook."

Coach Dresso handed the tape recorder back to him and extended his hand. "That's not all," he said. "You're back on the team, too. That is, if you're willing to play with us again."

"Oh, you bet I am!" Scott cried. "What about Bill?"

The coach shrugged. "I'll have to talk to him," he said. "Come on. I'll drive you home."

Scott sat in the car like a robot, picturing the look on his father's face when Scott told him the good news.

"Want me to come in with you?" Coach Dresso asked as he stopped the car in front of Scott's house. "To help smooth things over?"

"Thanks, but I think I can handle it, Coach," Scott said, trying hard to hide his excitement. "See you later!"

He slammed the car door, then ran up to the house.

"It's over with!" he said to his father, the first person he saw after he closed the front door behind him. "I got the guy who framed me!"

His father stared at him, silent.

"It was Bill Lowry!" Scott said excitedly. "The right guard for the Greyhawks!"

"You have proof?"

"You bet!" Scott took the tape recorder out of his pocket. "It's all on this," he said. "Jerilea Townsend let me borrow it. I caught Bill cold."

"I don't believe it!" his father whispered.

His mother and sisters came in from another room. They stood behind Mr. Kramer, gaping

141

at Scott as if he had just appeared from another planet.

"He stole Kear's wallet, too?" Mr. Kramer asked.

"Yes. He figured people would think I stole the money to buy more pot." Scott's eyes watered. "I — I've got a team again!" he cried.

"Scott, I'm sorry I doubted you," his father said quietly. "I really am. Will you forgive me?"

Scott looked at him and smiled. "Of course, Dad," he said and gave his father a tight hug.

That evening Scott called up Jerilea and invited her for a yogurt at Dan's Yogurt Shoppe. He was anxious to tell her the news, too. They met there at seven-thirty.

"Here you go," he said, returning the tape recorder to her. "It worked."

Jerilea's eyes widened. "You caught the crook?"

"Uh-huh."

"Who was it? Anybody I know?"

Scott nodded. "Bill Lowry."

"Bill Lowry? Oh, no! Who'd ever dream he'd do a thing like that?"

"I didn't," Scott said. "I was sure it was some-one else. It was lucky for me that he spoke up when he did — before I ran out of tape!"

When Scott got back home, he had barely sat down when he got a phone call.

"Hi, Scott," said a familiar voice.

"Kear?"

"Yeah. I just wanted to say . . . I'm sorry. For not believing you, I mean. I wanted to, but . . ."

"Forget it, man," Scott said. "It's all over with. And we're pals again, right?"

"Right!"

"Hey, do you know what happened to Bill?" Scott asked.

"No. I guess we won't find out until the game on Saturday," Kear said. "I sure wouldn't want to be in Bill's shoes."

"Yeah, you wouldn't. Don't forget — I *was* for a while!" Scott said.

When Saturday rolled around, Scott found himself feeling more anxious than excited about the game against the Royals. He wasn't sure how Rick and the other guys would feel about his being a Greyhawk again. At least he knew Kear was on his side.

The moment he reached the park, he spotted Rick and Sid Seaver eyeing him. His heart pounded as he went directly toward them and stretched out his hand.

"Hi, Rick. Hi, Sid," he said. "I'm sorry . . ."

"That's okay," Rick interrupted. "You had your reasons. Glad to have you back, Scott."

"Thanks," Scott said.

Every other member of the team shook his hand, too, and welcomed him back. Everyone but Bill, that is. Bill was nowhere to be seen.

"I had a private talk with Bill," Coach Dresso explained to Scott as the rest of the team warmed up. "After I told him about the tape, he confessed. Then he said I picked on him too much. I told him I didn't criticize him any more than I did the other players. And the criticism was meant to be constructive, to help him to do better the next time."

"Is he off the team?" Scott asked.

"Of course. I booted you off, didn't I? And

this time I had real proof. I couldn't give him just a slap on the hands."

Somehow, despite the suffering Scott had endured since that marijuana had been found in his duffel bag, he felt sorry for Bill. Scott knew what it was like to be a man without a team. But he understood the coach's decision. Unlike Coach Zacks, Coach Dresso played by the rules, and that was why Scott preferred being on his team. But maybe, he thought wryly, Bill would like to be a Cougar!

"Hey, just like old times!" Kear said as he and Scott ran out on the field together.

"Yeah!" Scott replied, feeling like shouting out loud — shouting something crazy — so that the whole world would know how good he felt. But he restrained himself and just said, "Man! It sure is good to be a Greyhawk again!"

20522

F
CHR

Christopher, Matt.

Tackle without a
team.

QUAKERTOWN ELEMENTARY SCHOOL
123 S 7TH ST QUAKERTOWN PA